What
is this buzzing,
do you
hear it too?

Books by Luigi Malerba

THE SERPENT

**WHAT IS THIS BUZZING,
DO YOU HEAR IT TOO?**

What
is this buzzing,
do you
hear it too?

LUIGI MALERBA

translated by William Weaver

FARRAR, STRAUS & GIROUX
NEW YORK

contents

[vii]

10.

A black dog? Yes, a black dog. See here she said a black b
[55]

11.

The ballooners and the army cameramen had set up camp in the
[60]

12.

I'll ask you a question, Rosa said, let's just see how you a
[66]

13.

Keep talking fly-killer because the truth, if it exists, soo
[72]

14.

Rosella looked at me and didn't say anything, she sat there
[80]

15.

Sunday is a day to spend in the house I go about on my bicy
[86]

16.

The lady of the villa said why what is the Necrophila Funer
[92]

17.

They say he was wandering around the Pavona Plain and frigh
[96]

18.

How wonderful, Rosalma said, we're all alone you and me in
[102]

19.

I see a black meadow and a green bird the High Tension wire
[107]

30.

The Heavens on the other hand were blue. There was a white
[165]

31.

The police have found this pair of eyeglasses near the Fosso
[169]

32.

I'm not coming to Rome you go if you want to go there. They
[173]

33.

You go along the paved road that crosses the Valley of Aricci
[178]

34.

Giuseppe has died too the fly-killer of the City of Albano,
[182]

35.

I went to the sea and I stayed for hours and hours on the b
[187]

36.

Now cripes you're exaggerating. THE BEACH ATTENDANT TOO. A
[193]

37.

I see a little procession beyond the hedge, a black automobi
[198]

38.

Giuseppe, dear friend, no dear friend we're not friends any
[203]

What
is this buzzing,
do you
hear it too?

1.

Am I dreaming, or do you hear it too? This buzz, this buzzing. Where is it coming from? From Heaven, from the Earth? Take it easy, it's nothing. Then it's my ears. No, no, it's coming from outside. This buzz, this buzzing isn't my ears. All right I'll tell you what it is, it's the Santa Palomba tower of the Italian Radio, and

THE POPE IS SPEAKING.

Maybe you're right, I heard some Latin words, he said *magis magisque* just this minute. Of course, the Pope speaks Latin, what do you expect him to speak? That's his language, it's like French for the French, for centuries and centuries the Popes have spoken Latin. But it's a dead language, if you please. The Pope speaks the way he likes. All right it's Latin then but it

[3]

can't be the Pope who's making all this buzz, this buzzing. I tell you when the Pope loses his temper it's worse than a thunderstorm. A swarm of flies is flying in the Heavens over Pavona, it's the flies if you ask me. No, you're wrong, it's the Pope speaking over the Vatican Radio, wait and see.

The air was heavy and dusty like the days when the American planes were about to arrive and bomb us. You could hear something from far off, the air would start vibrating, the dust and the wind rose together, suddenly, the trees shook like leaves, dogs began to run off with their tails tucked in as they do before an earthquake. Were these old memories or were the planes really about to arrive? Here come the Americans with their bombs, arriving from Sicily, the Flying Fortresses.

This buzz, this buzzing is the airplanes. Take it easy Giuseppe the war's been over for many years, it's peacetime. All the same this buzz comes from the Heavens, this buzzing, it's airplanes. Then they must be the Italian planes, the jets from the military airport at Pratica di Mare, on a training flight. You can hear the boom when they break the sound barrier. Don't be afraid, they don't do any harm, they're just out for a stroll in the Heavens, so let them go.

Now I can feel the Earth shaking under my feet, can't you feel it too? This business of the Earth is a funny thing, the Pratica di Mare jets fly high in the Heavens. You want to bet it's really tanks making all this buzz, this buzzing? There I recognize it, I hear the sound of tanks, they're coming from the sea. They've landed between Anzio and Nettuno and they're about to arrive. Over there behind that hedge I see something moving. It's them. See here, you're mistaken, well let me be mistaken.

[4]

Giuseppe, my dear friend, you're sleeping, how can you sleep with all this buzz, this buzzing? I'm a heavy sleeper, not even cannonfire wakes me, not even bombs from airplanes or the boom of jets breaking the sound barrier, if you please.

In a minute the ball of fire will come and it will destroy everything in its path. There it is. It's coming, it's coming. And it will have the shape of a dragon. No, see here you're getting mixed up with the Bible, it happens from time to time, getting things confused. I hear the ball of fire arriving in the form of a dragon and it will flood the whole Plain. Maybe you're getting mixed up with the Great Flood, dragons don't exist any more nowadays and balls of fire exist only in the future, who ever saw any balls of fire? What about Hiroshima? You're right, I won't say another word, I'll cut off my ears, no, wait, don't do that.

This swarm of flies was flying around the Santa Palomba tower of the Italian Radio, the air was vibrating the Earth was trembling, let it tremble. I'm tired of this buzz, of this buzzing. Here come the flies, they're coming they're coming, down from the Heavens. There must be millions and millions, the Heavens are all black,

IT'S FRIGHTENING.

What do you plan to do? I don't know but I'm certainly not going to stay here and let myself be eaten up.

There's plenty of space for walking in the Pavona Plain, square mile after square mile, there are near places and far ones, roads that go up and others that go down, you can advance and then come back, you can also stand still if you want to stand still. A person can take walks alone or in company, if he finds the company. You can leave or arrive, proceed at a run or move slowly, you can run away. Giuseppe, my dear friend, that might be the best thing. Where to? It doesn't matter, just far away. Because of that business which took place near the Mediaeval Tower.

They say the grass was stained with blood and they found a knife in the middle of the meadow. It surely didn't pop up from the Earth by itself. Only mushrooms pop up from the Earth when it's the season, in autumn when it rains. Especially in chestnut woods, but sometimes also in meadows, the so-called meadow mushrooms.

Run now, Giuseppe, get up and run, it's very late. Late for what? I have nothing to do. You can't stand still, Giuseppe, the World runs and you must run with it, you can't stop. Otherwise you'll miss your appointment. But I don't have any appointments I don't have to be any place, there's nobody waiting for me. Making an appointment is easy enough. Do you have some change? Make a phone call. Get moving, don't stand there like a stick. If a man runs it means he's running away from something and I don't want to run away.

I HAVEN'T DONE ANYTHING.

That's not possible you're sure to have done something.

2.

That way the airplanes don't crash into it. That's why they put the red lights on the Santa Palomba tower of the Italian Radio. They always turn them on at night you can see them from far off. A few miles away there's the military airport at Pratica di Mare where the planes land and take off, the jets. They put the red lights there on account of them. Around the tower there's the Pavona Plain with its ups and downs its hills and valleys and, farther on, its mountains.

We're fifteen miles from Rome and yet there are abandoned houses, it's like the desert of the jungle, the pampa of the savannah. If I look around me I don't see anything, this Plain is a

TABULA RASA,

but according to the Land Registry and the Maps of the

Military Topographical Institute there are many roads and many paths, wells mines springs cemeteries ruins cement walls and dry walls factories, but where are these factories? Towards Latina there are factories but here there's nothing. Cisterns fences monuments, but what monuments? To Mazzini or to Garibaldi? Everyone's fed up with Those Two. Bridges, if there are bridges there should be rivers too, what rivers? Where are they? Beacons, where are these beacons, I don't see any, and beacons exist to be seen. Here the Map says spring, but where is this spring?

THERE'S NOTHING HERE.

On the Map everything has its symbol and every piece of Land has a Christian name and a surname but nobody knows anything about it. Every so often the Map says Santa Maria in Fornarola or else Madonna dei Ritardi, Santa Maria della Vertigine or San Gaspare del Bufalo, but why buffalo? There are so many animals in this World and I haven't seen a single buffalo around these parts. Or else the Map says Quarto del Cuore, Quarto delle Ginestre, Quarto Massimetta, but where are these Quarters? I've never seen them and I've never heard anybody mention their name.

So I say cripes what are they up to inventing these names and these Quarters, the men at the Land Registry and the Military Topographical Institute, what are you up to inventing names for every piece of Land and then not telling them to anybody? You'd make a dog laugh with your names and your symbols. I say this especially for the Topographical Administrator, who signed the Map of the zone, a certain Macioti, and for the captain who carried out the General Survey, Captain Guidicini, and for First Topographer Luccichini. First among whom? Why are you First Topographer? Who are the others? Where are they? How did you manage to become the first? You must be one of those men who get to be first thanks to political pull.

The Map says that the Geographical co-ordinates are co-ordinated to the Ellipsoid oriented at Monte Mario, Rome. But what is this Ellipsoid? Speak clearly and we'll all be better off.

I look around the countryside and I see nothing, there are no marks on the Earth, but the Map says that the Italian Grid was made according to the Gauss-Boaga projection, International Ellipsoid. But where is this Italian Grid? I don't see it. And who might this Gauss-Boaga be? To begin with, is it one man or two? Who are you, both of you? Go bury your head(s), too, and we'll be better off, or else change your profession(s).

A MAN WAS KILLED HERE

and you didn't notice a thing, if you please. You with your projections and your grid. There's a man lying dead in the middle of the meadow near the Mediaeval Tower.

People who live in the Plain after a year or two are overcome by desperation and they go and live in other places. Some of them stand it a little longer but then they run off too. Those who don't run off become commuting Romans they go back and forth to Rome on the train. They all abandon the

Land and it's best to abandon it, they say so openly. They do just the opposite of what the Bible says when it says be fruitful and multiply and the Pope says it too in his talks over the Vatican Radio.

The people of Pavona are small of stature, they are descended from the slaves sent here to work the Land by the Ancient Romans. The Ancient Romans sent out slaves in other words prisoners of war from the Levant who were all small of stature. In addition to being small of stature they are also nasty, you have to go around all the time with a stick and a knife, and if you own a pistol, with a pistol. You can have unpleasant encounters at night and elsewhere. Better to try to mingle with nature, with the Earth, with the bushes with the darkness of the night, at night. Around every corner there could be somebody who's waiting for you in order to stick his knife into you. If you meet somebody at night it's probable he's a tramp, a murderer, but if you're going around at night you too might be a tramp, a murderer. Two murderers meet in the night, often one of the two is murdered. Often, that is every now and then.

Very well, I also go around at night looking for scrap metal. I'm always going around. I mean if you have lead pipes and copper pots or also copper pipes and lead pots, if you have a few pounds of brass I'll give you two hundred lire a pound, I buy brass taps and copper wire and also copper taps and brass wire, for copper I'll pay you four hundred and fifty. I also buy waste paper empty bottles rabbit skins wool rags and other rags, I buy rubber bakelite broken mirrors and unbroken burnt-out light bulbs, in other words

I BUY EVERYTHING.

Even Italian human hair. It's used for wigs and is better than Chinese. Also gold and silver if I find them but my specialties are zinc lead copper brass, if you please. But watch out, I don't want stolen goods.

Often the people who sell scrap metal are thieves who tear the copper wire from the High Tension lines. They'll be electrocuted one of these days, you'll be electrocuted. Or else the gas pipes, they work all night and pile up hundreds and hundreds of pounds of lead. They'll be asphyxiated one of these nights, you'll be asphyxiated by the gas if you're not careful.

If a person buys these metals from a thief he immediately becomes a fence, whether or not he knows he's dealing in stolen goods. I buy only from those who have a house in other words a fixed address. If you don't have an address I won't even speak with you. I never buy anything in the streets, I can't run the risk of having my license taken away from me.

There are also professional fences I have nothing in common with which. I deal with wholesalers from Rome from Naples and from Terni on a commercial basis. Everybody knows me, I am

GIUSEPPE KNOWN AS GIUSEPPE,

I am a professional merchant, I buy zinc lead copper brass, I pay my taxes, my name is also in the Albano telephone directory. I also buy empty bottles rags and waste paper. Waste paper is only a figure of speech, often waste paper is books and newspapers.

3.

It was one of Italy's hottest days. I was walking in the Sun in the middle of a meadow and the meadow was deserted. There was tall grass, every now and then my foot sank into one of the holes in the terrain. Go on, all right I'm going on. I was walking in the Sun in the middle of a meadow, I had shoes with very thin soles the ones I wear in summer namely canvas shoes. A bit farther on there were vines and olive trees all in a row, a persimmon a High Tension pole an apple tree. Go on don't stop, all right I'm going on but I'm walking slowly, under the Sun in the middle of a meadow.

My feet hurt in the canvas shoes it isn't like walking on a road, there are the spiky stubs of grass mowed in spring. They're hard. There isn't an inch of shadow anywhere to take refuge from the Sun, I'd gladly stop to take off my shoes and smoke a French cigarette. But I need a stone to sit on and smoke. Giuseppe, there aren't any stones around here. All right I can start digging in the Earth and find one. If I keep digging.

I was walking in the middle of a meadow, the grass was tall, alfalfa. In these parts alfalfa grows better than clover and doesn't exhaust the Earth which is already exhausted by nature. Alfalfa is better than clover and trefoil, if you please. On go on, Giuseppe. All right I'll go on, all of a sudden I felt something under my foot. It must be a tree trunk, strange though in the midst of a meadow in the Pavona Plain where there are no trees for square mile after square mile. If it isn't a tree trunk it must be something resembling one. I bent over to look down, cripes

IT WAS A HUMAN LEG.

Let's not exaggerate, I'm not exaggerating in the least and attached to the leg was the body of a man with his throat cut, lying on the grass in the middle of the meadow.

Well and then what? Then nothing, I took to my heels and ran off. But why were you walking in the middle of the meadow, where were you going? To the Mediaeval Tower, to the shepherd's. Giuseppe, my dear friend, for two years now the shepherd hasn't been living in the Mediaeval Tower there are Americans in it now. They had it restored and they come to spend the summer months there, halfway between Rome and the sea. It's a husband and his wife, they have four children. No matter how mixed up a person might be he couldn't mix them up with an Italian shepherd. You can get even more mixed up than that with a dead man at your feet, if you please.

A cat with a dog, a dog with a newspaper, a newspaper with an umbrella, but where are there any umbrellas in the middle of a meadow in the summer with the Sun? An umbrella when it's raining.

Giuseppe, dear friend, tomorrow all the newspapers will talk about it on the page devoted to scandals, well let them talk. People will begin to gossip, well let them gossip. The police will cause a lot of confusion, well let them cause it. Sometimes they've confused the murderer with the victim, this is something I don't like much in other words I don't like it at all.

The murderer strolls off along the streets and the victim is there groping inside a tunnel and he doesn't even know if there's a hole at the other end as the Pavona priest says from the altar on Sunday mornings. Eyes are no use in the total darkness and neither are eyeglasses, he feels a great cold in his bones, he sits on the track and waits for the train there's nothing else he can do. If I knew this I'd have brought a wool undershirt and a candle to make some light with which.

Giuseppe, dear friend, at this point it's better for you to stand up and start walking again. All right I'll start walking again if you promise me that at the other end there are gardens with flowers and deck chairs and when I arrive I'll be surrounded by people and I'll spend my life or rather my death chatting. See here Giuseppe

DEATH IS REALLY NO PLACE
FOR CHATTING.

I was walking in the middle of the meadow and the meadow was deserted in other words there was nobody there. All right even in the desert there could be somebody I'll give you an example, in the Sahara. There are Tuaregs, Tebus, and there are also Arabs who go around on camels I mean on dromedaries. Then there are monkeys lions hyenas and jackals and many kinds of serpents and cockroaches. Skip the cockroaches, for the police you have to have witnesses. I've already said there wasn't anybody how many times do I have to tell you there wasn't even a dog?

Giuseppe, my dearest friend, you can hunt for witnesses. All right but I can't go to Africa to hunt for them in the Sahara Desert. You go to Africa I'm not going to go there to die in the desert and get myself eaten by the hyenas. Almost everybody who ever went there is dead, along the camel tracks there are hundreds of white men's bones, if you please. And as if the hyenas and jackals weren't enough the desert is full of birds of prey the famous African vultures, you don't even have time to die before the flesh is stripped from your bones in a minute.

YOU GO GET YOUR FLESH STRIPPED OFF

in Africa in the Sahara Desert hunting for witnesses.

I feel something inside the handcuffs, it must be my wrists. Better give the police a wide berth, I don't want anything to do with them. I'd almost retrace my steps in other words I've never been in that meadow near the Mediaeval Tower where the shepherd used to live and the Americans live now. Has something happened? I don't know anything about it, see here certain things simply don't happen. There are things that happen at night, others that happen in the daytime, and still

[16]

others not at all. There are those that happen now, others that will happen next month, many have already happened in the past, but

MANY THINGS WILL NEVER HAPPEN.

Some of these things could perhaps happen one day with a bit of effort, a person stands and waits for generations and generations and still they don't happen.

If it's a question of a crime, it's just as well that way, but what sort of things are these things that never happen? There's no telling how to find out. In that case, I'd like to know this, what becomes of these things that have never happened and will never happen? What place do they have in history? Is there any hope for them? I mean at a certain point do they too finally happen or not? Do other things happen in their place? Anything is fine if it happens in place of a crime provided it isn't something worse, like an earthquake. In 1908 thirty thousand people died in the famous Messina Earthquake. Thirty thousand people is no handful, if you please.

In any case if an earthquake absolutely has to happen, let it happen far away like that one in Turkey where more than two thousand five hundred Turks died but here in Pavona they didn't even notice it. A crime however is noticed by everybody. The suspicions, the gossip. The police go into action, they begin their questioning, I don't want to be questioned. Giuseppe, my dear friend, in a case like this it's wise for you to run away I already have run away. It's wise for you to run farther, go very far away. There are people who have crossed Russia running away like

[17]

during his famous retreat. It was winter and snow was falling, the soldiers died of the cold and yet they were running away at forty degrees below zero Centigrade. They were being chased by the Cossacks on horseback, this is no joking matter.

Nothing, I have nothing to tell. I wasn't walking in the middle of the meadow and the meadow wasn't deserted. There wasn't any tall grass and every now and then my foot didn't sink into the holes in the terrain. Go on. I didn't have shoes with thin soles I mean they weren't canvas shoes. A bit farther on there weren't vines and olive trees all in a row, not even a persimmon tree a High Tension pole an apple tree.

My feet weren't hurting luckily in the meadow there weren't the spiky stubs of the grass mowed in the spring. I wouldn't have stopped gladly to take off my shoes and smoke a French cigarette. I don't smoke. I wasn't looking for a stone to sit down on, I wanted to remain standing. It's useless to insist I don't like staying in the shade, you stay there if you want to stay there.

I wasn't walking in the middle of a meadow, there wasn't any tall grass in other words it was all mowed, in summer. Go on, Giuseppe, all right I'll go on backwards. All of a sudden I didn't feel something under my foot, I didn't bend over to look down, cripes luckily it wasn't a human leg. Attached to the leg there wasn't the body of a man lying on the grass in the middle of the meadow. I didn't see it with my own eyes, it was impossible to see it because it wasn't there. But where were you going? I wasn't going anywhere and to be precise I wasn't going to the Mediaeval Tower. Go on. Naturally I didn't take to my heels and run away. Then you didn't see anything. I didn't see anything. All right then, you may go. You may go, perhaps.

4.

THE POLICE DON'T COME BY ACCIDENT

if they come it's because somebody has told them to come. I
didn't call them you can be sure of that, I have no connection
with the police I mean the only connection I have is that when
I see them I look the other way because I don't want to see
them. The police have their informers, their spies. The spy
says for example see here so-and-so is bringing meat into the
village that was butchered illegally, the butcher. The police
informs the Food Board. The Food Board arrives and fines the
butcher who is butchering illegally so as not to pay the tax.

Sometimes I mean very often these informers are men of the
underworld who have got out of jail. They have a very black
police record. They spend whole days sitting at the Bar

Centrale in Pavona and every now and then they get up and make a telephone call. At the end of the month they go to collect their money from the police like a government employee who works for the Government.

The informer says they've found a dead man murdered in the middle of a meadow near the Mediaeval Tower. The police immediately start arriving, they've already arrived with their squad cars and their jeeps, they walk back and forth in the meadow. They've begun searching in the grass and behind the hedge. They walk back and forth on the Italian Grid and then they start all over again because they haven't found anything. Maybe not even they know what they're hunting for but they're sure they'll find it this thing they're hunting for.

Why don't they arrest somebody? There are plenty of people to arrest. Giuseppe, dear friend, the police move cautiously. But where do they move cautiously? They're going in the wrong direction, they run and run and really they're asleep, if you please. See here the police are light sleepers, the slightest thing wakes them up. See here the police have clever tricks, sometimes they pretend to be asleep and instead they are keeping an eye open. You notice how many people are arriving? The police study them one by one.

Along with the people from Pavona in the meadow the Romans also arrive driving by on the road that goes from Albano to the sea. They stop their cars at the side of the road and walk on the meadow they are all sweating. Also a priest has arrived dressed in black.

The people walk in the meadow, they light a cigarette, they come closer. They want to see it. People are morbid in certain circumstances. Stand back, the police say,

And above all silence we have work to do. Instead the people talk all the time, they say you know it's a mistake it isn't the murdered man who comes back to the scene of the crime it's the murderer. He doesn't have eyeglasses but it's as if he had them, they found in his pocket a pack of French cigarettes, nobody knows his name, if he were alive he would be terribly embarrassed to have died like this, they burn the clothes but I'd like to know about the watch and the eyeglasses, the fingerprints of the dead man are of no use to anybody.

The carabinieri are better than the police, for crimes they say the police are better than the carabinieri, they saw a man on a bicycle black in shape and color, it wasn't a dog it was a man with a cap on his head, at night between a man and a dog there's very little difference, for that matter also between a dog and a man, however they really ought to brush the flies away.

There are people who can't stand the sight of blood whether it's their own or other people's, they say a man's beard keeps on growing even afterwards, fingernails the same as hair, in Egypt the dead all become mummies because of the dry air and the sand, in some cases the eyes explode suddenly, this is the first time I've seen a really dead man, they should at least send the children away and the bicycles.

There are ways and ways of dying, yesterday he was going around on his own legs and now he isn't anybody and tomorrow still less, there are animals that smell the odor of blood from a distance, I didn't even know blood had an odor, a woman is pretending to cry you mustn't disturb her, a dead man is nothing compared to the heat these days, it's only an optical illusion.

A bit of hurly-burly before the eternal silence, mind you it isn't silence but eternal cold, we should ask a priest, priests know as much about it as we do, I wonder if this eternity really exists, you mustn't get too many ideas about death, we can still have a few laughs about it.

TALK TALK

while you're alive because when you're dead you won't talk any more.

Some of them go away but others continue to arrive, owners of the houses and the villas in the neighborhood, servants gardeners farmhands. But Giuseppe, what are you talking about? There are no houses and there are no villas around here. If there aren't they can be built with a little cement and a few bricks, there are contractors who also work with reinforced concrete and there are those with prefabricated parts who can put you up a villa in two months right to the roof. Another month for the frames and the details. If you're willing to pay you can also have a tennis court and swimming pool, there are the Esther Williams kind with plastic lining and illumination. They're beautiful. You can also have a bowls court with special sand. And big trees around to hide everything, lindens eucalyptus oleanders and stone pines.

Giuseppe, dear friend, there aren't any trees either around here. If there aren't you can plant them, you just have to call on special firms like Sgaravatti and Ansaloni they can transplant even very big trees a hundred years old. These firms take care of everything, they have trucks cranes bulldozers and everything required. The trees are sold with a guarantee I mean you pay only when they've taken root otherwise you don't pay anything.

With this system you could make a park, a pine woods, you could transform the Pavona Plain into a forest. In the middle of this forest the heat isn't so bad now and the air is purer because the eucalyptus trees have purified it. The leaves on the branches are so thick and interwoven that the Sun has a hard time penetrating like in the African Jungle. There you find the oddest plants in the whole Vegetal System. In the depressions little lakes are formed full of fish who allow themselves to be caught and in the branches there are birds of every species who do nothing but chirp. Under the trees huge flowers grow with bright colors like those of the

EARTHLY PARADISE.

Naturally there are also snakes and other animals, certain enormous spiders that weave their web from one tree to the next and certain ants that proceed in columns like columns of soldiers. You have to pay careful attention if you don't want to end up being devoured by these ants they're very voracious.

On the road next to the meadow an automobile stops very long and very black, an old man gets out and the chauffeur walks behind him and says to him don't walk all that way on foot with this Sun and this heat Admiral because of your heart. And the Admiral says to the driver don't worry about me because my heart has no fear in other words he talks like the Bible when he talks of his heart and it too says my heart has no fear. But then the chauffeur says what the devil is an Admiral doing in the middle of a meadow. An Admiral all at sea.

5.

The police bent over to look down into the grass of the meadow and then they picked up something in a handkerchief. In certain cases the police use a handkerchief so as not to erase the fingerprints they are very important in finding the murderer. Now the police are acting mysterious but everyone has found out anyway what they picked up in the middle of the meadow, a knife. Perhaps the knife was used by the murderer, the fingerprints will tell, if there are any. It isn't mine that's sure, I never carry knives I've never had a knife. I don't even know what a knife looks like, if you please.

The purple alfalfa flowers are spotted with red, apparently the blood spurted a long way as the newspapers will also report. A crime can be reconstructed in all its details and in fact the police are lying down on the Earth and then they get up and begin to run, they repeat the whole scene from the start calculating the time with stopwatch in hand there's not much to calculate. They started arguing in the meadow, a policeman says, and then they had a fight, that is the murderer murdered the victim. It happened at night. I always say

NIGHT IS A BAD PLACE TO ARGUE.

Now let's talk about this knife. What brand is it, in other words where was it manufactured, where was it sold and in what shop? If there are any, also the fingerprints but sometimes the murderer puts on gloves to commit his crime. The police won't have an easy task. In this neighborhood there are several shops that sell knives, there are also knife factories, farther on towards Latina.

Around Latina there's the Industrial Area where many factories went up in the Period of the Boom. They make everything, drawn metal plastic objects detergents medicines ceramics bathtubs household appliances, also knives and various items of hardware. They also make spoons and forks, if you please. These factories are all interconnected, that is they exchange their by-products and from these they produce other products and with the by-products from them they make still more products, ad infinitum. They don't throw anything away. So almost all the factories say

MANUFACTURERS OF PRIZE-WINNING THIS THAT
OR THE OTHER

and Related Products. By that they mean the by-products.

Even now when the Boom is over these factories go on working and advertise themselves and their products a lot.

[27]

There are colored signs along the roads saying Legnoplast Metalfer Suometal Ferrobeton Metaltex et cetera. These factories that sprang up in the Period of the Boom create incredible combinations with wood metals plastic materials synthetic fibers and an infinity of other things. We're in the vanguard, they say, we make things nobody else knows how to make. A sign says for example Bertolaso Rain Inc. this is a factory that makes artificial rain in every season, Pontina Floors on the other hand makes floors old-fashioned and modern, Bertolazzi Gears makes the best gears in the World. There is a Factory for Brakes of every kind, for braking, and the Ovital Farms which produces fresh hen's eggs produced by industrial methods. But a hundred yards farther on a rival sign says Buy Your Eggs directly from the Hens.

They worked miracles around here in the Period of the Boom and they're still working them. Supertenax Ultrafluid Maxitext Optifon Extraflex. One sign says Joy of Rome Ltd. Another sign says S.I.S. that is Superior Italian Society. But superior to whom? Make yourselves clear on points like this. There are also factories that manufacture structures, Ghira Inc., and manufacturers of framework for manufacturing other factories, that is from one factory another is born, it's all a chain. Now that the machines have started they can't be stopped any more.

There is a Straw Hat Factory, which means craftsmanship on the industrial level. There are foreign factories from far away like the American Abbot and the German Lorentz, and there is also Viterbo Enamels and everyone says what did they come here to Latina for? Why don't they go back to Viterbo we don't need them here. Go back to Viterbo and you'll be better off. The same applies to Genoa Foundry and Glazers, why don't they go back to Genoa? Go back to Genoa and you'll be better off.

Other colored signs say OR WO but nobody can find out what this OR WO is and there are others that say Molliconi but nobody knows who this Molliconi is. Who are you Molliconi? What are you doing? The signs just say Molliconi and nothing else.

At the entrance to the Industrial Area at Latina there is one sign bigger than the others which says

MANUFACTURERS CHOOSE THE PROVINCE
OF LATINA,

exclamation point. Here there is the Southern Italy Development Fund and in fact the manufacturers all rush to Latina like locusts. Locusts are all very well but you, Molliconi, must tell me who you are and what you're doing.

The knife's blade was stained with blood but the police stop and think before they say this is

THE MURDER WEAPON.

From the wound the police can determine how long the blade is, how many centimeters and even millimeters with breathtaking precision. The police when they set their minds to it are very precise, the Police Laboratory. In certain cases the murderer is left-handed and uses the blade backwards, in certain cases the murderer has a special ability in handling knives and then the police already have a clue in hand. Many times the murderer has been discovered in this way and he has turned out to be for example a butcher. In other cases it was discovered that the murderer was a surgeon. A surgeon when he cuts knows where the muscles are the bones the tendons and the other obstacles, he cuts with a sure hand, he's done nothing else all his life.

The blood will be analyzed. The police analyze everything, you never can tell. They count the red corpuscles one by one under a microscope. From the analysis of the blood they can discover for example whether the victim was drunk at the moment of the crime, if he had any diseases, or whether he died in good health, how long ago the crime took place. The blood is one of the elements for reconstructing the crime and discovering the murderer.

BLOOD TELLS NO LIES.

However you have to know about it otherwise it can also confuse things. There are people who lose their heads when they see blood, there are people who faint away because they can't stand the sight of it. For example I can't bear to see blood and I can't even read about it in the newspaper. Giuseppe, my dear friend, everybody has blood, you have blood too and you have to get used to it.

There's another thing however. Some say that this knife found in the grass, this knife that should be the murder weapon and that the police have sent to Rome for analysis, is a knife without a blade. Then the blade can't be bloodstained, if you please. It will be very hard to establish what sort of blade it is if this blade is no longer there, or where it was manufactured, Germany Sweden Italy, the length the thickness, straight or curved, double- or single-edged. Everybody says funny about the knife, even the police say funny about the knife without a blade. This complicates the investigation, it's an advantage for the murderer.

The police however still have the handle at their disposal, I mean from the handle you can tell what kind of knife, the shape the brand the length. From the handle you can tell what kind of knife just as from the tail you can tell the breed of a dog or another animal.

The handle can be of various types and various shapes, of wood bone metal mother-of-pearl, nowadays they make knife handles of plastic materials that resemble wood bone metal mother-of-pearl. Even of plastic that resembles leather, or of leather that resembles plastic. Certain knife handles are worked by hand like those ancient ones from Toledo which is however more famous for the blades than for the handles. In fact people say

TOLEDO BLADES

are famous all over the World.

In Rome there are still certain artisans behind Piazza Navona in Via del Teatro della Pace who work with the burin, they're incredibly skilled and they can fit a whole scene from the Bible into a square inch. The sacrifice of Abraham. The Ancient Chinese were also specialists in this work of precision and miniature. However more than anything else they worked with jade, from jade they carved the handle and also the blade. Jade is a very hard stone that is worked with a diamond tip. They

[31]

worked it even before diamonds had been discovered God knows how they did it. Maybe they worked jade with jade.

On the handle of some compact material, for example an unengraved metal, bone or plastic, the police can easily find fingerprints. If a murderer leaves fingerprints on the murder weapon, he's had it. Sooner or later they arrest him. Theoretically the police could arrest him with mathematical certainty, all they have to do is take the fingerprints of all the inhabitants of the Earth.

But this is no simple thing to organize, I mean the police would have to have at their disposal a Great Universal File where all of us are on file with our fingerprints, including the police themselves, naturally and including also the Pope and the President. Not because the Pope and the President can commit a crime, not any more. It's only a question of principle, otherwise you start making distinctions. With the electronic brain method the matter would be quite simple, not all that simple.

But did the murderer leave his prints on the handle? The police have sent the handle to Rome and in a short while we'll have an answer. The Police Laboratory works even at night. I'm very curious to know, but Rosa says it's impossible because the knife found by the police in the grass didn't even have a handle. This is another advantage for the murderer who, if he exists, must be very clever.

The police won't be able to count much on this knife for their investigation, I wouldn't like to be in the police's shoes, poor things. Rosaria says there aren't only fingerprints in this World and she's right too there are lots of other things. The Radio is broadcasting *Songs You Love.*

[32]

6.

The Pavona butcher has very small eyes but that doesn't necessarily mean he's a murderer and vice versa. He has a receding forehead and a receding chin but that doesn't mean anything, there are plenty of people who have foreheads and chins like his. His ears are larger than normal and I notice he moves them when he speaks, nothing wrong with that.

He looks hard at me as I say you know how to handle knives, with a knife in your hand from morning to night. Solingen. It's my trade, he says, I'm a butcher. Nice trade you have Mister butcher. If you don't like it you can go away. Nice trade I said I mean it, it must give you a certain satisfaction standing there all day with a knife in hand.

From outside I saw the sign that says

FIRST-CLASS BUTCHER SHOP

beef and horse meat. So you sell horse meat too I sell what I please he also sold horse meat. However I don't sell frozen meat. He looked at me sideways and said may I ask what you want? If you're a customer what can I do for you, otherwise you're bothering me because I'm working. I laughed chuckled. You're a butcher, I said, and you also sell horse meat. Well, well, horse meat.

I walked back and forth in the shop with my hands clasped behind my back. Go away, the butcher said, go home. Instead I am staying here and I'm not moving, I mean I am walking back and forth. The butcher had a knife in his hand, he began to huff and become agitated, he gave me black looks. You have a knife in your hand, Mister butcher, watch what you're doing. Don't get any ideas about threatening me, you know you can be reported for threats with a knife it's a serious charge, an infraction of the penal code, if you please. The butcher stood there with the knife in his hand, he looked at me.

First and last names, I said. The whole village knows my name anyone can tell you.

AND HOW'S OUR POLICE RECORD?

Come on answer. He's trapped, I thought, you're trapped, butcher. And he took me by the arm, go away, he said, go home if you have a home. I have one but I'm not going there. Are you from the Food Board, he asked, or are you from the Internal Revenue? Why don't you speak up? We can come to an agreement, he said.

By chance do you go around at night on a bicycle? I asked.

[34]

Sometimes I go around with one yes. This bicycle is black, it's wise for you to confess. Explain more clearly, the butcher said, what I'm to confess, the color. Your hands are still blood-stained, show me your hands. The butcher looked at his hands. Are you from the Food Board? he asked. We can come to an agreement in two minutes. How much do you want?

A woman comes in and says one pound of rump steak, Signor Giuseppe. Cripes, I say, is your name Giuseppe? Big discovery you've made, the butcher said, my name's been Giuseppe for more than fifty years, fifty-two. This is something I don't like much, I mean I don't like it at all, this business of his name being Giuseppe the same as mine. It's something that doesn't concern you, the butcher said, my name is Giuseppe and it always has been.

You'd be wise to confess, I said. Explain yourself a bit more clearly and tell me what I must confess. You know very well and instead you pretend not to understand. Then you're from the Food Board? I'll give you money, if you'll just go away. He was very arrogant. Spill the beans, Mister butcher, you'll feel better afterwards. I feel fine and I told you I don't believe it, you must have something too in your chest where your heart should be. There now I understand, he said, you're

A PRIEST DISGUISED AS A CIVILIAN

or a monk going around to hear people's confessions if you want I'll give you an offering but afterwards get out and don't show your face in here again.

I'm not a priest or a monk, not at all, Mister butcher. I called him Mister butcher. Every now and then I called him Giuseppe like me. And he struck blows with his knife, he cut pieces of meat on the counter. I see you're very precise in your cutting, Giuseppe. He had lighted a cigarette and was taking long drags on it. He was very nervous you're a bit nervous, it seems to me. Mind your own business or else, if you're from the Food Board, I've already told you we can come to an agreement. Or are you from the Internal Revenue? In either case we can come to an agreement.

I went up to him and said to his face, why don't you confess? It's the wise thing. You know this place that's called the Mediaeval Tower? Of course I know it, I was born in Pavona, some Americans are living there. All right, I said, some Americans and then what? I really don't understand, Giuseppe said, what's going on in your head what you want. You wouldn't by any chance be pretending not to understand? Now I understand you're from the Food Board, the butcher said. And I said you think you're very clever, you're playing it clever.

I swear I don't understand I don't understand a thing, he said, if you'll speak out clearly you'll be doing me a favor. I don't do favors for a character like you. Murderer, I said, but only in my mind. I was getting angry, this is no joking matter.

The butcher looked at me and then he said I've heard there are certain priests who go around in disguise to talk with people, to convert them. Sometimes they even start swearing to gain people's confidence. Are you one of them? Or if you ask me you're from the Food Board. If you really are a priest, see here father, speak up clearly what do you want without

[36]

making such a mystery of it? He called me father like when you talk with a priest.

Let's not drag things out, Giuseppe said, tell me who you are, from the Food Board a priest? He really believed it. And I said first you have to confess if yesterday evening you were at the Mediaeval Tower, what you went there for, if you lost something in the middle of the meadow. You aren't by any chance missing a knife? Why don't you count them? I still don't understand he still didn't understand. What knife? I'm not missing anything and I said make a good examination of conscience, butcher.

I work from morning to night, father, you know I kill many animals and I kill them with my own hands. It's a funny thing, he said, sometimes it doesn't seem like anything to me, other times it's like being a criminal. There, I said, finally we've got to the point, now he's beginning to confess. That is, Giuseppe said, sometimes I wonder if all those animals added up together in the end won't count the same as killing a human being. I know it's an ignorant question however I think about it all the time, add them up animal after animal, in the end. Just look at the problems he invents, I said to myself, this butcher. If by any chance you're from the Food Board, forget it and just pretend I haven't said a thing.

I can tell you honestly, I said, in my view, cattle horses hens you can kill all you want and then add them all up but they'll never come out like killing a human being. There's a big difference, if you please.

HAVE YOU STUDIED YOUR CATECHISM?

Did they baptize you? Have you been confirmed? Of course, the butcher said, but I have another question well ask it. The soul for example, Giuseppe said, are you sure that we have this soul? I mean us human beings.

What kind of talk is this, what are we talking about, Mister butcher? And he said personally

I DON'T FEEL ANY SOUL

in other words it seems to me I don't have anything inside. See here, I said, as far as that goes we're all equal I mean between you and the Pope there's no difference, the difference is with animals. We human beings have a soul. And if by any chance it isn't there? he said, when we're dead we'll lie there like so many fools.

But you privately, he said, what do you think about it? That is, do you feel this soul inside or don't you feel anything? I feel something, I said, a strange buzz, this must surely be the soul. Tell me a bit about how you feel it, the butcher said, all spread out to infinity or else like a little cloud, like the puff of smoke from a cigarette? Of all questions, I said, of all the crazy questions, I'd say it's a bit more like a little cloud however I could be mistaken on this subject.

Let me go away, it's getting late. Stay here another ten minutes or so, Giuseppe said, do me this favor, I'll pull down the blind and we'll stay here and discuss things. I'll come back another time, don't worry I'll come to see you and with that I went out along the main street of Pavona the bicycles of the evening were passing.

I was pedaling uphill towards Albano. Don't tire yourself out with your bicycle, Rosetta said, all right I'll buy a motorcycle for which. A Mosquito. As I pedaled along I thought of the crime at the Mediaeval Tower, this butcher is worse than an eel for slipping away. But if I set my mind on it, I'll make him fall into the net I'm more stubborn than the police who are stubborn as a mule. And I am more stubborn than both, than the mule and the police put together. Mules live in the mountains, Giuseppe, they're beasts of burden, I've never seen a mule around here. If you haven't seen one you've made a mistake by not seeing it, a mule.

The Radio was broadcasting *An Hour with Sibelius* on the Third Program, I don't like this composer. Why an hour? Half an hour was more than enough for him.

7.

Many old people go to take the cure in Switzerland at Geneva and at Basel where there are these clinics that specialize in old age, with monkey hormones. The secret of youth. Youth is all very well however be careful with these hormones.

YOU WILL BECOME MONKEYS TOO

without realizing it, one day you'll wake up like that character who couldn't recognize himself in the mirror any more. He said who's this monkey what's he doing in my house. Go away. He went to Africa to Kenya without saying goodbye to anybody and was never heard from again.

My cure on the other hand is a very ancient one like Royal Paste and like certain vapors that come out of the Earth. Unfortunately in its natural form it's incredibly wicked. You have to acquire a taste for it and that's not easy. I arrive at Rosalma's house with a little bunch of rosemary and I say you have to chew this so the milk will change flavor. Luckily she likes rosemary she's glad to chew it.

Rosemary is easily found in any season, it's an evergreen plant. If by chance however it can't be found I start hunting for it everywhere and in the end I find it. If I absolutely can't find it then I hunt for it somewhere else. It takes patience and perseverance as the Pavona priest says on Sunday mornings. Even when it seems impossible to find and everybody says nothing doing no rosemary, I don't give up. I hunt for it until I find it.

Sometimes I cover many miles on foot under the Sun or in the rain, I'm capable of walking all night and in the end my arms droop to the Earth, it's dawn and the first workers go by heading for their work in the factories of Latina. Their faces are still sleepy and they yawn on their bicycles, they don't feel like going to work, they're right. However they have to support the family in other words the wife and children but there are also those who aren't married and they work all the same against the day when they will have a family. Others go to work and then spend the money foolishly, they're free to spend it as they like.

Even when everybody says absolutely not, I insist and in the end I succeed in finding the rosemary to take to Rossella. They say seek and you shall find I mean the proverb says so, perhaps. Often instead a person seeks and seeks and in the end never finds anything or else he finds something entirely different from what he was seeking. A man who was looking for rosemary found an unexploded bomb bedded in the sand. He had to call the specialists from the Army Engineers to have it defused.

They shouldn't leave these bombs lying around after twenty years there are still some in the center of Milan and other cities, in the countryside and buried in the sand on the Italian beaches. At least they should put up signs saying

UNEXPLODED BOMBS.

There are some in the sea also. Two months ago a fishing boat blew up off Anzio because of a drifting German torpedo. Four fishermen died, if you please.

However I've always found rosemary to take to Rosmunda. Sometimes I've had to work hard but the important thing is to find it in the end nothing else counts. If on the other hand I simply don't find it, well nobody's going to die over it. I don't think anybody ever died through the fault of rosemary. Through the fault of a bomb or a torpedo. You have to chew this, I say, this rosemary.

Seated at the window Rosalia had started chewing the rosemary, I roamed around like a madman to find it you roamed around like a madman, she said, where did you find it? It doesn't matter where I found it in a restaurant in Albano the Belvedere, mostly tourists passing through go there. A terrace with a view over the Plain fresh mushrooms and game view of the sea in the distance reasonable prices, not all that reasonable.

The milk came down slowly, I was looking out of the window at the people going by. Giuseppe, my dearest friend, what people when there's nobody there? Then I'll look at the countryside with the cows grazing on the meadow and you let me look. But what cows on the meadow? Maybe you're mistaken and thinking of the Po Plain, there they have cows on the meadow grazing. They're three hundred miles away, you can't see them at such a distance in other words you're mistaken well let me make mistakes, cows on the meadow.

I'm hot, Roselda said, she was in her slip, then she had taken off her stockings, she undressed but what are you planning to do? We can lie on the bed, she said, and I said no we'll remain seated here by the window. I am aware of the window, she said, the bed is much better. She had begun to unbutton my jacket you should undress too leave my buttons alone, I said. See here the bed is the most fun of all, in bed we can do all sorts of things the way we used to do a long time ago. That way you give me energy in one direction and in the other you take it away from me, I said, no sweetheart.

The milk came down very slowly. What's happening, I said, it's about to end. Apparently I've dried up, for that matter you knew it can't last forever, I know I knew I've always known. That's why I told you to drink beer you have to drink plenty, that's what all women do when they have to nurse they're drunk from morning to night. I don't like beer, all right you don't like it but then you want me to die. It's too bitter to the taste. I'll bring you whatever you like, I said, Swiss beer Dutch Danish German the English kind pale or dark or even the Italian which is pretty good.

I drink milk and I eat cheese they're good too, she said, I can't stand beer. See here, I said, the slogan goes

HE WHO DRINKS BEER WILL LIVE
A HUNDRED YEAR.

[43]

A hundred years is no small amount, if you please, a century. It's too long for me, she said, I'll live as long as I can and then I'll go off. All right you'll go off wait a moment before you go, I mean drink a little beer the more you drink the better it is for both of us. I like wine, she said, then close your eyes and swallow the beer thinking of something else, of wine.

Sometimes, she said, the ducts close up with the waning Moon and vice versa the milk starts again with the waxing Moon that is we have to wait until next month. In a month they'll have me under the sod, if you please. Come to the bed, she said, what should I come there for look my cock is fast asleep. Even if I lie on the bed nothing will happen. I'll bring you a case of a foreign brand. Wührer. It turns my stomach, all right it turns your stomach meanwhile I'm on my way to

THE ETERNAL COLD

just because you don't like beer.

She had sat down on the bed and was looking at me, then I haven't explained how can I explain it to you? Don't explain anything to me, Rosalinda said, either you come to bed or I won't drink any beer I don't like it.

8.

I am walking slowly along the dusty road, I am coming from Rosina's house at Casale Abbruciato. I am returning to Casale Abbruciato slowly on the dusty road. I am pushing my bicycle it has a flat tire. It must be a nail, that happens often I mean it had never happened to me in all the years I've been going around on a bicycle. Giuseppe, my dear friend, it can't be just an accidental nail, that nail was put there by somebody to make you go on foot.

A MAN ON FOOT IS AN EASY TARGET.

I shut my eyes and walk with my eyes shut, I pretend to whistle, I look up towards Heaven. Skip Heaven, Giuseppe, for the moment. There at the curve in the road there is an oleander bush there's a man hidden behind which.

You'll have to defend yourself somehow. All right somehow, I put my hand in my pocket as if I had a revolver too. He'll try to shoot first but I'll be all ready and waiting, I'll be the first to shoot the way they did in Chicago at the time of Al Capone when men shot each other point blank in the streets.

The clock says three-twenty and Rosalba is waiting for me. I walk in the dust of the road silent and light as a breeze, I hope not to make myself conspicuous. Somebody wants to eliminate me from the scene of this World, if you please. I take my handkerchief and I wipe the sweat it is pouring from my forehead. But why doesn't this character move? I advance pushing my bicycle, calmly, not all that calmly. Giuseppe, you're trembling. It's not me it's the handlebars that shake then what are you waiting for to change them? If you also change the frame the wheels and the chain it'll be like new.

Now I see him moving among the leaves, cripes he's coming straight towards me. He has a cigarette in his mouth and the smoke is mingling with the dust of the road. A puff of smoke then another puff, he's coming forward hanging his head. My last thoughts are passing through my mind.

There he's coming closer, he's still smoking his cigarette, he sends the smoke out of the radiator. The water has started boiling all of a sudden and the cap has blown off. Obviously the fan isn't working well. Better an air-cooling system then, like the Volkswagen has. Water-cooling caused trouble also for the machine-gunners in the First World War. Then the machine guns were water-cooled like the Fiat so-called Mod. 14. During battles the barrel became overheated, the water started

[46]

boiling, it all vanished in steam. In winter the opposite happened, the water froze. You had to shoot willy-nilly, otherwise it became hard as ice and the machine gun jammed. Water-cooling has many drawbacks as you must have noticed.

Be careful, Giuseppe, he'll run over you. Wait, don't shoot. Let him come closer and then shoot him point blank in the center of the forehead. A bullet between the horns will knock him cold, his forehead is his Achilles' heel. But you must take care not to miss, it could be fatal for you. In any case, before shooting take shelter behind a tree trunk or a light pole. But here there aren't any trees and no light poles. Do you let that worry you? If there aren't any here there must be some elsewhere.

Hurry, take shelter otherwise you'll end up being gored on his horns. You know how Granero died he died with a horn in his eye and he was only twenty. His parents wanted him to study the violin and he wanted to be a torero. In the plaza in Madrid a bull by the name of Pocapena ran him through at the comenzar su faena de muleta, le derribó, le volvió a meter la cabeza una vez caído, empujándole hasta debajo del estribo de la barrera, donde le corneó horriblemente, metiéndole un pitón por un ojo.

You'll end up like Granero if you don't take shelter. To the Earth, throw yourself down on the Earth, see if there's a manhole where you can take shelter from the bullets. There it's making a nose dive. Keep still, don't move, maybe it can't see you. You hear how it whistles? That's the engines. You feel this wind? It's the propellers. Still, keep still, maybe he'll confuse you with the grass of the meadow. But there isn't a blade of grass here there's only dry Earth. It's the same thing,

[47]

if you keep still he'll confuse you with dry Earth, the important thing is for him to confuse you with something.

You remember during the war? One day you were strafed first by the Americans and then by the Germans along the Nettuno road. It's a miracle you're still alive. Around you there were dozens of dead bodies, men women horses, even a dog had been hit and now he was there alongside the others with his eyes staring and his tongue hanging out, he was the most dead of all. You risk meeting the same end as that dog if you don't take shelter right away.

There he's coming, he's coming. But this is water. It's raining. Then don't waste any time, get your umbrella open. Are you ashamed to open your umbrella? There's nobody who can see you and besides there's nothing to be ashamed of, you have to take shelter somehow. Or would you rather catch a cold? You know a cold can turn into pneumonia with no effort at all. All right, today pneumonia is cured with penicillin, it isn't a disease that frightens people the way it once did, however it strikes the lungs all the same, if you please. Don't you have an umbrella? Then why are you ashamed of opening it? Open it without fear.

There he's coming, this time he's really coming. He's laughing apparently I make him laugh. I'll start laughing too but in my laughter fear is also included. I feel his cold breath on my face I don't want to feel it. I shut my eyes I open them I shut them again. I can't see anything but what is all this noise in my ears? Giuseppe, dear friend, it's your heart beating. All right, my heart's beating that means it works. I open my eyes again, I look around there's nothing there's nobody, so much the better.

[48]

I start walking again towards Casale Abbruciato. You can't hear the birds chirping in the branches, you can't even hear the cicadas. Yes you can hear them I don't hear a thing what you can't hear the cicadas? I don't hear them try to hear them they make a very rasping sound, you absolutely must hear them I don't hear them. I only hear the voice of the Radio which is broadcasting

LIGHT CLASSICS

on the Second Program, I don't like it. You don't like anything. You're right I don't like anything, cripes would you mind telling me then what is it I want?

9.

Rossanda was looking at me I don't understand what you're looking at, I said, I'm looking at this handkerchief you've tied around your neck I just put it there for decoration. For decoration there are scarves of colored silk or colored wool, she said, this is a handkerchief for your nose let me see it it's stained with blood. All right, I said, it's stained with blood I have a little scratch, very superficial.

How did you manage to scratch yourself? I didn't notice anything I mean I woke up this morning with my neck bleeding. I did nothing but run all night that is I was running in my dream I don't know where, maybe I was running away. Rosangela undid the handkerchief, there's a very thin little scab which came away in tiny pieces, what were you running away from? I don't know a thing about it now I don't even remember a word, these things happen in dreams. There was a meadow, I think, a road a tower a hedge a ditch a sun-baked bed of stones.

This little cut, she said, hidden under the handkerchief you don't want to talk about it no let's talk about it then. She looked at me closely, it looks as if it had been made with a razor blade or else with a pocket knife. You ran a nasty risk, you know that

THE NECK IS VERY DANGEROUS.

All right, I said, the neck is very dangerous, then so is a toe, the whole human body. The neck if I may say so, she said, is attached to the head. That's where the veins pass, through the neck, and the breath and the spinal column.

The little scab had come away, it had left a faint scar. Rosella massaged me with her fingers on which. Right on the neck, she said, I'm thinking go ahead and think you're free to think what are you thinking about? I'm thinking about that man, he also had a cut on his neck and I said they cut his throat, if you please. We were talking about that old man found dead in the meadow near the Mediaeval Tower. You can't compare me to a dead man, I said, because of this little cut, but she said you have a cut on your neck exactly like him.

These are natural symmetries, I said, millions of them occur in the whole Universe, there must probably be another Planet where at this moment two people like us are talking about a little cut on the neck and he is saying these are natural symmetries millions of them occur in the whole Universe. Not so natural as all that these symmetries, she said, what do you

 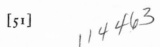

mean by natural, natural for whom? Natural according to nature. Then, she said, I'd like to know what is the nature of nature you want to know too much. Maybe it's only a coincidence, I said, pure chance. Giuseppe, my dearest friend, nothing occurs by chance not even when the cicadas start singing.

Now that the scab has come off, Rossana said, I'll wash your handkerchief, with blood you need cold water and no soap. All right cold water and no soap but now let's think about other things, there are so many to think about more than those that exist in the World. This is the beautiful thing about thought it has great freedom of movement in all directions. You can guide it or let it wander, pursue it or drag it after you like a dog on a leash, with a little push it can surpass the speed of light, this is no joking matter. Then tell me what I must think, she said, think of whatever you like, freely.

For example, I'd like to know if this cut is yours or whose it is, I don't know if I make myself clear you've made yourself quite clear whose do you think it is? The neck is mine so this cut must be mine too I mean this little scar. Strange you didn't feel any pain and now you're cured and feel normal as before. All right I feel normal as before, not all that normal. I feel something odd in my head, I said, I mean I feel as if it's been cut off like in the days of the guillotine when they cut people's heads off. They cut them off even before they invented the guillotine, with the axe. Chinese Emperors cut off prisoners' heads after battles. Caligula had prisoners' heads cut off when the prisons were too full.

As a rule in ancient times everyone preferred to die with his head cut off rather than be hanged. In certain cases the condemned people were first hanged and then decapitated, in England at the time of Anne Boleyn. She too ended up decapitated. A certain Lord Capel wanted to keep his hat on his head while they cut it off but they told him no, they were right. A very skilled English executioner was able to cut off two heads with a single blow but another one in order to cut off the head of a certain De Thou had to bring down his axe eleven times.

In other words, I said, I don't feel my head on my neck very firmly I mean I hardly feel it at all. So it happens that my thoughts have a very hard time keeping together, they fly off every moment into the atmosphere. And the situation gets worse

WHEN THE WIND BLOWS.

How my thoughts fly when the wind is blowing in the Plain. I hold on to my head with my hands, my neck doesn't support it at all well. If the air is the seat of straying thoughts, that's where they tend to scatter in the midst of the currents of which. The neck inside the collar, a collie is collapsing, the colloquy of the colonel, collyrium in the eye, Albano in a colossal cholera wave, the collard greens in the colon. You can make connections between one thought and another if you want to make them.

Giuseppe, my dearest friend, don't worry about thoughts, be content that your blood goes on circulating in your veins. I'm content all right, however I feel a great movement in the air around here, I don't know what's happening. You know in certain cases

[53]

the slightest thing is enough to make it go hog wild. Not such a slight thing, Rosanna says, a man with his throat cut. What do you think that is compared to the mystery of the whole World?

You hear those blows beating like hammers? That is the pounding that keeps it in its natural course. I don't feel a thing, these hammer blows. You don't feel them, you don't want to feel them. They're like the thumping of a motor, like the pulsations of the veins due to the heart and she says forget about the heart, it goes on its way by itself and you let it go on its way, the World. All right I'll let it go it would go on anyhow.

10.

A black dog? Yes, a black dog. See here she said a black bicycle no she said a black dog, I'm sure of that. She may have been confused in the dark. You can't confuse a black dog with a black bicycle in the dark. A dog is a dog, almost always. A dog has paws head tail and a central body, so has a bicycle a central body and the Pavona newsstand lady could very well have confused a dog with a bicycle and vice versa. Yes but it isn't the dog that counts, you have to find the man who was riding the dog I mean the bicycle. Why don't you hunt for this charatcer with the black bicycle he hasn't been identified yet.

The police are spinning their wheels, wasting time. They say keep back give us room to work. They look for footprints on the ground, they take a lot of pictures, they telephone Rome. The police take orders from Rome from Headquarters.

Go ahead and take pictures, I say, there's plenty to take pictures of. Mind you green doesn't come out well in pictures, the green of the meadow on Kodachrome. Often the police never listen to anybody, they bumble along blind and deaf, they simply don't know where to turn. Keep hunting, telephone Rome, take pictures. You'll arrive at a nice fat nothing with your methods.

THEY DON'T KNOW A THING IN ROME.

I sit down in the meadow, I keep my eye on the police and I stare hard at them. I look at them and I don't say a thing. Then I stand up suddenly and say go back to your homes and you'll be better off.

Giuseppe, dearest friend, do you have any suspicions at least? For the moment no but they'll come to me, it doesn't take much to suspect. For example a black bicycle belongs to the fly-killer from Albano he's always riding around from morning to night. Let's find him right away this fly-killer. There's a swarm of flies moving about the Heavens over Pavona just stand still and wait, where there are flies is where he'll be, and when he comes you must question him.

Giuseppe, dear friend, you too have a black bicycle and this being the case you'd be wise to change the subject. On the contrary it doesn't matter if it's black it can be painted another color. Green, for example, red or certain colors somewhere between green and red, all you have to do is choose. There are excellent enamel paints in all colors. Once people talked about German paints, now you can use the local ones as well they're even better.

[56]

Keep moving, the police say, haven't you ever seen a dead man before? They're hunting in the grass, God knows what they think they're going to find. What are you hunting for? They don't put any feeling into it you don't put any feeling into it. And so you can't find it this thing you're hunting for. The police work in cold blood on crimes committed in heat, this is why they mostly never achieve anything. For them all crimes are alike, they're incredibly cynical. Roselda says

I'VE NEVER SEEN THE POLICE CRY.

I haven't either.

The police don't want to arrest the fly-killer then arrest somebody else. Go to Rome, it's full of murderers. If they don't own a black bicycle they can buy one or else you can give them one. How much does a black bicycle cost it should cost about twenty thousand lire at the most and with all the money you have. Do you pay informers? Then you can also pay for a bicycle to give the murderer or else, with a little patience, you can find one who already has a black bicycle and his hands stained with blood, if you please.

In Rome murderers walk about freely, you meet them at every step walking in the street. Often your elbow grazes his, that is the elbow of a murderer. Those feet in those shoes that are climbing the steps of the underpass in Via Tritone are the feet of a murderer. When you mount the bus or go into a tobacconist's and say give me a pack of Gitanes, there's a man next to you who also says give me a pack of Gitanes. You don't notice anything but that man who smokes the same

[57]

cigarettes you smoke and who is there beside you at the tobacconist's counter is a murderer. Or at least he might be.

Also that little old woman with the astrakhan collar to whom you give your seat on the bus and she sits down and thanks you with a smile, when she was younger she killed her husband by strangling him. Nobody knows she did it and now when you see her she's a little old lady who will die of old age. She isn't a little old lady like all the others, she's a murderess. Rosalia says we can't go on like this any more like this. The Architect also complains and says I can't stand any more of these murderers there are too many. What about the police? The police are doing what they can in other words they're not doing anything there's nothing to be done.

Here in Pavona the opposite is true, murderers are scarce and policemen on the contrary are plentiful. People in villages inform on one another, they'll all wind up in Regina Coeli Prison if the police pay any attention to them and then the villages will wind up uninhabited, Pavona and Albano.

The police are shadowing me, they follow me at a distance, closely. Naturally they don't show themselves they hide behind a tree trunk a bush the corner of a house, if there is a house. Sometimes they crawl along on all fours in the ditch beside the road or behind the hedge, if there is a hedge. They have time to waste. Sometimes one of them follows me in a truck dressed as a truck driver, other times on a bicycle dressed as a cyclist. The police think I haven't noticed anything, on this score they are really naïve. If I turn around I don't see them but I know they're shadowing me. Rosmunda says well let them shadow.

They tell me sometimes the police follow a false trail in

order to confuse things, that is the murderer. The police disguised in civilian clothes. Sometimes they run here and there, other times they sit and wait, they watch the people who go by on bicycles. Provided the bicycle is black, if it's another color they don't even look up.

I run off pretending to be just out for the ride. I pedal in the middle of the main street of Pavona the so-called Sea Road which however is eight miles away, the Tyrrhenian Sea. They all look at me there's nothing to look at go ahead and look why are you looking at me? All right it's obvious that

SOMEBODY HAS MENTIONED MY NAME.

Giuseppe, dearest friend, who can it have been? I have my suspicions then speak out. I don't trust you you can trust me. Nobody, if you please, and besides tell me this you know who Judas Iscariot was? General silence.

11.

The ballooners and the army cameramen had set up camp in the Plain between Santa Palomba and Albano near Casale Abbruciato. Well come and look then, said Rossella, look at these madmen who go up in the air in balloons.

The ballooners and their balloons could be seen rising from the distance, they became very small in the Heavens and then they disappeared completely. The cameramen went up with their cameras and disappeared into the Heavens along with the ballooners. Lucky them. What they'll go and photograph isn't clear, Rosalma said, in the Heavens there's only air and you can't photograph air.

From the Heavens you can photograph the Earth, I said, and from the Earth you can photograph air I mean the Heavens in all their splendor, I mean you don't have to go up into the Heavens to photograph the Heavens. I paused to chat a bit between one feeding and the next. When the milk wouldn't come for a while I lighted a cigarette and she said I don't smoke because of the milk. A bit of nicotine doesn't do any harm, I said, smoke go ahead and smoke, however the milk isn't coming well I have to pull hard in proportion.

More ballooners and more cameramen kept on going up from the Earth, what are they up to? If you ask me they're plotting something, I said, what? I don't know for the moment. Will there be a long wait? That depends. Certain things happen immediately and others take years and years, I'm here waiting let me wait.

I CAN WAIT EVEN FOR CENTURIES IF IT'S NECESSARY.

I see the World changing around me, houses collapse, even whole cities and others are built in their place, men dissolve like licorice sticks. I'm here waiting. I don't bother anybody, I'm quiet and still, nobody notices me. Men pass me by all of them going some place, they hide.

I don't understand the way they talk any more what they say, they've all become foreigners these men who are around me, this posterity. What can they be saying? They seem a bit agitated to me. Something big is happening, I hear noises, I see them run off, take refuge underground. They slip into certain holes and disappear like ants. The noise increases, the air is hotter and hotter. What is happening? Cripes now I'm dissolving too like a licorice stick, if you please. Help me then, I'll do anything but don't leave me here alone. I'd rather be underground with you even if the Earth isn't to my liking.

[61]

YOU CAN'T BREATHE EARTH.

There another group of ballooners and cameramen is taking off. Lucky them. What are they looking for up there in the Heavens? Maybe they're just going up to look down, or maybe they're going up for pure amusement. I've heard it said that

THE HEAVENS ARE VERY AMUSING.

Not all that amusing, Rosetta says, when you're suspended in the air without anything you can lean on. And those soldiers, they don't know what amusement is. In certain cases, I said, amusement includes boredom.

Or else, I said, a war can't have broken out by any chance. I don't think so I'd have heard it mentioned. It could have broken out this morning, do you read the papers and listen to the Radio do you watch Television? On Television I only see the ads and the songs however if there was a war don't worry I'd have heard it mentioned. But in that case, I say, what have these ballooners come here for, and these army cameramen? What they're doing I can't say I see them go up but I can't tell you what they're doing, they're strange people and they do strange things. All right strange things, they'll end up disturbing the Architect, I said, up in the Heavens.

You'll see they're secretly waging a terrible and silent war, it's not like the days in Libya against the Bedouins when wars made a lot of noise. Leave the Bedouins alone, leave them where they are, said Rosaria, I mean in Libya. But then she said suddenly you're talking about Libya, see here that war against the Bedouins was a long time ago. Cripes you're right, but how old am I then? Shut up, you're very very old.

It's incredible the number of things that have taken to happening around here. These ballooners these cameramen, I don't know why I waste my time on them. What are you doing there with balloons, I said, balloons nowadays make a dog laugh, they're so antiquated they make a dog laugh. Ten thousand meters' altitude is nothing, a run-of-the-mill airplane, one of those that take off every day from Fiumicino, flies at ten thousand meters, and those that take off from the military airport at Pratica di Mare go very much higher.

In 1936 Stevens and Anderson reached an altitude of twenty-two thousand and seventy-six meters in a balloon. You can't go any higher than that. The day of the balloon is over, if you're not careful you'll end up caught on the Santa Palomba tower of the Italian Radio. The sentry looked at me and kept silent, he couldn't talk but I saw he was very nervous and was trying to look anywhere rather than look me in the eye. He had never heard of Stevens and Anderson.

Why don't you sit down and we'll smoke a cigarette? I said, and at the same time we'll have a nice chat. We'll talk of whatever you like, sentry, you say something to me and I'll answer you. I blew the smoke in his face to make him feel a desire to smoke. Then I held out my pack of cigarettes and I said sit down for a moment and let's chat. What do they intend to do up in the Heavens at an altitude of ten thousand meters? What do they think they'll find? Or what do they think they'll see from up there. They won't see anything. And when they're in the Heavens

[63]

DO THEY LOOK UP OR
DO THEY LOOK DOWN?

The sentry didn't answer. Maybe it's a new system of keeping an eye on what happens on the Terrestrial Crust? Have you heard something said or don't you know anything? There's plenty of talk around this neighborhood. You don't talk much but you have ears, sentry. What's being said? Or have they sealed your lips? Who was it? The sentry turned his eyes stamped his feet and didn't say anything. Where are you from? I asked, are you from Catania, in Sicily? You're short, sentry, you must be five feet three at the outside, you have black hair, you could be Sicilian or Sardinian. Also Calabrian or Apulian, as a rule short sentries with black hair are Southerners, if you please.

I had finished smoking the cigarette and I almost hadn't noticed it. I'm absent-minded. I took out the pack to light another. I smoke a lot, I said, I smoke one cigarette after another. I said this just to make conversation. They're good these light cigarettes made in Switzerland with American tobacco. Do you like cigarettes made in Switzerland with American tobacco? Or do you prefer the French ones made in Algeria with black tobacco? Mind you it wouldn't take me a minute, I'll go and buy you a pack of Gitanes, if you like. I could even get on my bicycle and in five minutes I'd be back here with the pack.

I puffed the smoke in his face to make him smell the odor of tobacco. Then you really don't want to sit down. Let's talk about it, I said. The sentry stamped his feet but obviously he

[64]

had orders not to talk, he kept his mouth shut and his lips shut. If you won't talk it's a sign you know something, sentry.

Why do they do these things without saying anything to me? Why do you always do things behind my back? I was beginning to insult him. Ugly idiot, I said, and he said nothing. See here you're pretty damn rude, see here I'll give you a kick and I acted as if I was going to give him a kick. It was obvious that the sentry was angry but he didn't move and he didn't say anything.

The ballooners and the cameramen continued going up. Lucky them. You can see their balloons shining against the Heavens they become smaller and smaller and then they disappear. I on the other hand have my feet on the Earth and my head on my neck, not all that much on my neck. Go ahead, I say, it won't do any good anyway. Nowadays there are rockets that go into the stratosphere, there are artificial satellites that circle the Moon and astronauts that circle the Earth. Go on up into the Heavens with your balloons, I say, as I pedal towards Albano.

YOU CLOWNS.

12.

I'll ask you a question, Rosa said, let's just see how you answer
what were you doing at the moment of the crime? Nobody
even knows exactly when it happened, yesterday evening.
What was I doing what do you think I was doing I was doing
nothing. Look nothing is too little, she said. All right it's too
little, then I could ask you the same question go ahead ask you
know very well I never leave the house. The police won't
believe that, there are plenty of fat women who are always
running around, they even make very long trips, they go from
one continent to another, like it was a joke, on ships and in
planes. There are plenty of fat people who travel in this
World. Do you remember Churchill? He did nothing but
travel. There are also the women in carnivals, the so-called
Cannon Woman who goes from one country to another

constantly. That may also be true, she said, but I'm not like the women in carnivals, like the so-called Cannon Woman.

You talk so much, she said, all right I talk so much, however at the right moment I don't say a thing, when it's time to be silent. It would be better, I said, to question these tramps there are lots of them in the area, and among these tramps there's also you, Rosalinda said, right in plain sight. All right then there are also the farm workers who hire out by the day, there are the workers in the factories down towards Latina, and the Romans who pass through going to swim at Torvaianica. Gardeners owners of villas servants chicken-farmers artisans and unemployed, if you please.

And then there are the two of us, if you don't mind. Let's speak frankly, she said,

AFTER ALL, SOMEBODY MUST HAVE KILLED HIM.

All right somebody I have nothing to do with him, this murderer. If the police get their hands on you, she said, do you have an alibi? If I'm not mistaken however I'm innocent, you're forgetting this little detail and she said that remains to be proved. All right I'll show you, I'll prove anything I want to. I light another cigarette, I smoke calmly, let me think, I said, and meanwhile I was smoking. Go ahead and smoke, Giuseppe, you have plenty to smoke about.

Now, ask some questions and I'll answer you. Let's begin by saying that I arrived here at seven-thirty in the afternoon towards evening and I found you watching Television. Telefunken. No dear, you have to be precise with the police what was I watching? All right then you were watching the commercials you watch them every evening. Not at all yesterday evening I didn't see the commercials there was a play. Then let's say there was a play I don't remember the name of which. See here the police are terribly fussy, mind you afterwards they'll want to know the plot. It can be invented, I said, they're all the same anyway.

They may be all the same as you say these plots, Rosina said, but they're not all the same in the least. The police watch Television and they don't let themselves be deceived so easily. All right then you can't tell the plot of this play, no matter, I don't understand what you bought a Television set for. I leave it turned on all the time, she said, but I don't pay much attention to it. It goes on by itself singing and dancing, I pass back and forth in front of it in the house, sometimes I sit down there in the armchair and I fall asleep. If I've been bored when I wake up I say

WATCH OUT OR I'LL CHANGE CHANNELS,

that is I watch a bit on Channel One and a bit on Channel Two, and this way leaves you with no plot to tell.

All right apart from Television we can say whatever we like. For example yesterday evening in your house it seems to me there was a dog. I understand a dog, she said, what sort of dog? And I said any sort is good, it's only a dog for telling the police about.

Then let's say a mongrel stray dog with a red coat and a black nose who just came here by chance. The red coat and the black nose, I said, I don't like, it would be better a red nose and black coat. Let's think about it a moment, she said, see here if you want my opinion it had a red coat and a black nose like I said before. No it had a red nose and a black coat, if you please. But what dog are you talking about? About that mongrel stray dog who came by chance into your house yesterday evening, I remember him well he had a red nose and a black coat. You see you're mistaken?, she said, he had a black nose and a red coat I can see him before my very eyes as if it were yesterday. And I could swear on the contrary that he had a red nose, I said, and a black coat. Maybe you've got him mixed up or else you don't remember him well, that mongrel stray dog had a red nose and a black coat. I also gave him a piece of bread because he was hungry, she said, I remember clearly he had a black nose, no a red nose, I said, and a black coat.

If we can't agree, she said, it's going to be a nasty business with the police. All right then why don't we chase him away with a kick this mongrel stray dog with a red nose and a black coat? As you like, she said, however we're chasing away a dog with a black nose and a red coat like I said. I'm capable of throwing him out of the window, I said, you know stray dogs sometimes have leprosy and she said no rabies more than leprosy, let's not exaggerate. They can very well have leprosy too dogs carry around every sort of disease just like human beings, if you please. Where do you think the big epidemics come from they come from dogs. From rats more than dogs, Rossanda said, and I said if we like they come from both the Encyclopaedia Britannica says so too.

If you ask me it's the wine that makes you mix these things up, she said, yesterday evening you drank a bit of wine you're not used to it. All right a bit of wine to tell the police about, a bit of white wine from Frascati. Red, there's also red wine from Frascati. No mind you it was white I'm absolutely sure of that. And at a certain point you got drunk, she said, all right I don't know what's best for me to say to the police but in this case it's white wine because white wine goes to my head more than red wine, if you please. And she said, the alcoholic content is the same even if the color is different, it was red. And while you were drinking let's say you dropped the bottle on the floor. Then I dropped a bottle of white wine on the floor. Red wine, she said, and as you picked up the pieces of glass you cut your finger, the tip. All right I cut my finger too bad for my finger, however the wine was white, maybe you're getting it mixed up with the blood from my fingertip.

Red it was red I should know what wine is drunk in my house, it was red. When you come right down to it, I said, red or white isn't it the same thing? White resembles red very closely and vice versa, they're almost the same. No dear, red and white are two very different colors. Then, I said, let's wait for the police to come question us, we can decide calmly red or white there isn't all this rush. No we have to know which it was. You want to know this minute? Better this minute than elsewhere, in Regina Coeli Prison.

Now see here, I said, if they come to question us we can talk about the finger in other words we do have something to tell them my finger cut by a sliver of glass from the bottle, what's the need of knowing the color of the wine that was in which?

A CUT FINGER OUGHT TO BE ALIBI ENOUGH.

Perhaps a leg would be better, Rosangela said, the police are never satisfied. All right a leg, I said, I don't much like that. Legs are for walking with only one leg you can't even pedal. Then go on foot, she said, no dear I'm not going to go limping around with only one leg, if you please.

I was pedaling towards Albano, I was whistling. Be careful, I said, with that whistling. I mean there might be somebody spying on you, better turn off the headlight. I was pedaling up hill, I was whistling. Giuseppe, what's this sweat pouring off your forehead? It's the uphill road. Would you mind saying where you're going what for? I'm going to have myself bandaged, I have to go to the pharmacy I cut my fingertip on a sliver of bottle.

Look at the cut I gave myself, it would be better not to have fingertips. Giuseppe, dear friend, compared to interplanetary travel what's a fingertip? All right compared to interplanetary travel, still it hurts. Even compared to the eclipse of the Sun a fingertip is nothing, even compared to Regina Coeli. And I said leave Regina Coeli right where it is, in Rome.

13.

Keep talking fly-killer because the truth, if it exists, sooner or later comes out. The fly-killer kept talking, they call me, he said, and I arrive with my pump and my drum of liquid molasses mixed with D.D.T. Where I pass by the dead can't be counted. By the millions, like in wartime. Men to me are just so many flies.

Keep talking fly-killer. I wage this war, he said, I hate flies. I can pump molasses and D.D.T. for hours without tiring, walls tree trunks electric poles hedges bowling greens and tennis courts yards gardens of houses and villas. Where you find all these things and all these houses I don't understand, I said, here in the Plain there isn't anything, it's a desert worse than the Sahara, however if you do find them you're right to de-fly them it's your trade.

They call me to the villas and the farmhouses down in the

low land that stretches towards the sea at Torvaianica. In that area the flies are nastier because of the pressure which on the contrary is higher. The lower the land the higher the pressure and vice versa. The higher the pressure the nastier the flies and vice versa.

Sometimes they call me to Torvaianica Tor San Lorenzo and Lido di Lavinio, the fly-killer said, where the Romans go in the summer to bathe in the sea. All those naked people, he said, the flies come running. And he said naturally,

FLIES HAVE A SWEET TOOTH FOR HUMAN BEINGS.

All right they have a sweet tooth for human beings, however they prefer córpses especially if there's blood spilled on the grass of the meadow, on the purple alfalfa flowers. That is flies come running where there's blood, I said, they smell the odor from far off. That's absolutely true, the fly-killer agreed with me. We don't even smell it this odor and they smell it from miles away. Keep talking fly-killer because the truth, if it exists, sooner or later comes out.

Sometimes they call me to come de-fly a house. I arrive on my bicycle with my pump and my drum of poisoned molasses. I have to bring my lunch with me, they all keep me well away from the kitchen and from food in general. So I take a bag with a bit of cheese or salami and a bottle of wine. They keep me well away from the wine too on account of the poison. In the bag I also put a glass, they keep me away even from the glasses. They're right, D.D.T. is a powerful and deadly poison, after all. With these fly poisons, I said, sometimes it happens that a human being is poisoned too, by mistake naturally. The

[73]

fly-killer looked at me and said I know how to tell a fly from a human being.

Flies, he said, will become used even to D.D.T. It's happened already in Sardinia after the big anti-fly campaign at the end of 1940, in Denmark in 1944 and in Egypt in 1948. By now the Egyptian flies are completely immune, they burst out laughing at the smell of D.D.T. The same thing happens in Sardinia and in Denmark the flies split their sides laughing. That may be true, the fly-killer said, but for the present when I pass by, the ground still turns black with flies like a battlefield. All right like a battlefield, but meanwhile you're infecting the air with these insecticides. You'll end up infecting the whole Planet with your poisons.

Mosquitoes, I said, in the end have become stronger through D.D.T. and the cockroaches in South America have become twice their size since they've been given D.D.T. A breed has developed that is much more immune to poisons. You're fighting a hopeless battle, fly-killer, and meanwhile you're poisoning the atmosphere. Soon human beings will also start dying like flies, if you please. And the fly-killer said maybe they'll become resistant too like the Egyptian flies and the cockroaches of South America.

Keep talking fly-killer because the truth. I go into a villa and I say what needs de-flying? And they almost always say, the owner of the villa or the house, everything needs de-flying, the walls the plants the hedges the terraces the flowers and the garden, if there is a garden, the roses and the shrubs, if there are roses and shrubs, the swimming pool, the drainpipes and some say why don't we also de-fly the compost pile, if there is a compost pile. Or else we carry out only a partial de-flying

[74]

that is just the walls of the house and the tree trunks, if there are trees. And then he asks how much does this de-flying cost? It doesn't cost anything because it's the City of Albano that pays. Fine, he says, that is the owner of the house or of the villa, in that case let's have a

TOTAL DE-FLYING.

When they hear it doesn't cost anything they want to de-fly everything, even the roof and the Television antenna, of course. Then I put my cap on my head and I begin my de-flying, I pump the molasses and the D.D.T. which is a mixture that's fairly hard to pump when it's too thick I add a few quarts of milk from the Central Dairy. Sometimes I start singing.

Keep talking fly-killer. In the past I used to race my bicycle in the Lakes Circuit Race, then I broke a leg, I limped. Now I'm a fly-killer there are no others in the whole district of Albano, there's only you there's only me. You must have heard my name mentioned what's your name? Giuseppe's my name but everybody just calls me The Fly-Killer of Albano. What did you say, your name is Giuseppe? My name is Giuseppe, if you don't mind, the fly-killer said. Cripes, another Giuseppe whose name is Giuseppe. Nothing, I said, it's a strange business this name. I've been called that ever since they baptized me. It's nothing I was just talking.

But how many Giuseppes are we then? How does it happen, cripes, that I run into one every so often? These symmetries have always frightened me. One of these days I'll get angry and I'll wipe them out every one, there'll be a massacre, if you please. Giuseppe, dear friend, now you're exaggerating, a massacre. What fault is it of theirs if they're named Giuseppe? So is the President of the Italian Republic, and Mazzini and Garibaldi. All right Mazzini and Garibaldi I don't even want to hear them mentioned. Those Two.

So the flies arrive and light where they smell the molasses it's very sweet. They immediately start licking it I mean sucking it with their proboscis because flies don't have a tongue, they have a proboscis like elephants. From the way he talked about them you could realize he hated flies. He said

FLIES HAVE NO HUMANITY.

All right they have no humanity but what makes you think you're any better with your molasses and your D.D.T.? In a small way you resemble those people who ran the gas chambers, with your massacres.

Sometimes I arrive at a villa, he said, for the de-flying and they're all still asleep early in the morning. Then I start shouting and I get them out of bed. Wake up, I say, wake up the fly-killer's come. I go around a lot do you also go around at night with your bicycle and your molasses? That happens rarely, Giuseppe said, I travel mostly in the daytime, the flies are happy in the heat, they buzz in the Sun. Keep talking, fly-killer I'm letting you talk go ahead and talk.

Often I find piles of garbage and I say why don't you cart this garbage away? Are you actually trying to feed the flies? Still you haven't found a sure way of exterminating them, I said, while there are plenty of ways of exterminating human beings. I was trying to shift the subject to human beings. But

[76]

Giuseppe said the flies buzz among the pines, they buzz in the garden among the roses and the other flowers, and they go and light on garbage pile beside the gate. What gate? I said. Any gate, the villa gate. What villa? Any villa. I don't like you very much, Giuseppe, with all this chatter of yours.

Then they fly in through the window, he said, and light on the soup, they drown in the wine glasses. All right, I said, but whose wine is it, whose wine glasses? The proprietors', said Giuseppe. Who are they what are their names, these proprietors? Just proprietors, I don't know their names and I don't even want to know them, he said.

Sometimes crickets die and butterflies too from my de-flying yes indeed, he said, in certain cases even hens die. And human beings? I said, sometimes human beings die too if you please, then the police arrive and they find a knife in the middle of the meadow. I was putting him through a kind of interrogation. You didn't by any chance lose a knife some-where in the middle of a meadow? No, Giuseppe said, what knife? I use molasses and D.D.T. all I'd need is a compressor for the pump. All right a compressor for the pump, I said, but when you're moving around all day I'm sure you have a knife in your pocket, no I don't you're mistaken.

Here unfortunately they cling to the old methods. He says you take a glass receptacle with the opening wide towards the top and narrow at the bottom like the neck of a flask turned upside down and it ends in another receptacle also of glass. In this second receptacle you put some vinegar or some salted water the fly goes in and dies by drowning. They make me laugh, he said, with their vinegar and salt water.

Flies multiply by the millions in a week, in a short time

[77]

they'll invade the whole Planet, they'll eat us alive if we're not careful.

THEY WANT TO TAKE OUR PLACE ON THE EARTH,

that's what flies have in mind, yes indeed. And what about the Chinese, I said. Giuseppe seemed a bit confused I don't know what the Chinese have in mind, he said. They're yellow.

The City of Albano does what it can, poor thing, it's put out a sign that says

WAR ON FLIES,

it says don't leave fruit peelings lying around, don't throw wine dregs on the ground at wine-making time, that is after the vintage when they make the wine. But the flies, I said, come running especially where there's blood, they have a very sweet tooth for blood and for decomposing matter.

There's always decomposing matter around everywhere, Giuseppe said, around the houses but also in the middle of meadows in every season, little dead animals. Men too, I said, for example that old man who was found dead in the middle of the meadow and the blood on the flowers all around and the knife in the grass. There's a road near there they saw you riding along which. I ride where I please. You were on a black bicycle I had it issued to me by the City of Albano, I have to move from place to place in my line of work.

At times the flies come in swarms even from far off, certain special strains. And I said flies are all the same oh no they're not all the same in the least, Giuseppe said, there are thousands

[78]

of different strains. To the naked eye the differences aren't very clear, he said, like when an Italian goes to China the Chinese seem all the same but they're not really.

You're right about the Chinese, I said. But I can't tell one fly from another, they all seem the same to me. There's a swarm flying around in the Heavens over Pavona these days, flies that have come from far off, Giuseppe said, I took one to a professor from the Public Health Department in Latina and he told me what they're called. Keep talking, fly-killer, I said, tell me all about this professor. He looked at one under a microscope and then he said this is

THE FAMOUS NECROPHILA FUNERARIA.

Just a minute, I've heard it mentioned before, I said, it's the one that smells the dead from far off. Right, Giuseppe said, when a war breaks out or an earthquake then she comes, the Necrophila Funeraria. Sometimes two or three days ahead of time as if she could read the future.

Does she also come when there's a dead man in the middle of a meadow near a Mediaeval Tower, I said, or is just one dead man not enough for her?

14.

Rosella looked at me and didn't say anything, she sat there dazed she didn't move and she didn't speak, you want to bet she's dead? It takes a lot to make me die, she says, and so my thought must have slipped out of my mouth involuntarily. You're sitting there and you seem numb, I said, you act like an embalmed mummy. If you want to see somebody who's really completely numb who looks like a mummy from head to foot, she showed me the newspaper with a photograph all black with a black spot on top of another black spot and that was the corpse and the black all around was the meadow. Will you please print these newspapers better, it's all black, I said, you can't see anything. They feed too much ink into the cylinders of the rotary press, you feed too much ink in.

With these rotary presses the newspapers are very badly

printed, especially the photographs. You feed too much ink in and then you run the rotary presses too fast. Take it easy,

THERE'S PLENTY OF TIME,

there are centuries and millennia and you stand there and count the minutes. Look at the Pyramids and learn something. They made things calmly, the Pharaohs, and you waste your time to save a few minutes in getting out your late city edition.

You can't see anything here, Rossana said, but the police have good eyesight. They found something in the grass. All right, something in the grass, I said, I'm happy for them, not all that happy. What exactly? Exactly how things stand nobody knows. Maybe the knife, I said, no it isn't the knife. I mean they haven't found anything specific but something in general. That's not possible, the police aren't like Plato who talks about things in general. We have to know what this thing they found is this is no joking matter.

There are so many things that can be found in the middle of a meadow, it wouldn't by any chance be a lamb, I said, or else a yam a ham a dam or a clam? A clam in the middle of a field

EIGHT MILES FROM THE SEA,

Rosanna said. I mean, I said, somebody must have carried it there. Skip the clam, the wife of the marble-cutter of Pavona saw something glisten in the hands of the police, like a brass object.

[81]

Then, I said, it wouldn't by any chance be a tap a trap a clip a trip? A trip, she said, in the middle of a field? There's nothing strange about that, any place is good for tripping people, a meadow a sidewalk a paved street a square in Florence or Milan the corridor of the Hospital of Albano. All the same, Rosella said, I don't believe in a brass trip. Maybe you're right, I said. Maybe, I mean surely.

Now don't let yourself get into a frenzy, she said, all right I won't let myself get into anything don't worry. Maybe it was only a hinge from a door. Or else, I said, from a Commodore. See here you, can't find a Commodore all that easily in the middle of a meadow. Ships are on the high seas cruisers and battleships, that's where Commodores are, I don't think there are any in the middle of a meadow. All right you don't think there are any in the middle of a meadow there can be all sorts of things, one day they found a stone that had fallen from the Moon, I said, and it had made a big hole in the Earth. A Commodore can be anywhere, including the vicinity of the Mediaeval Tower, if you please.

In any case let's skip the Commodore, tell me what you please in the middle of a meadow. A pistol a pistil a pole a pile. A panther or a puma. What is a puma? A carnivorous mammal of the American Forest, I've never heard this puma mentioned, she said. Here the Zingarelli Dictionary of the Italian Language says slender body without mane and without tufted tail, I'm sorry it doesn't have a tufted tail poor thing. The Dictionary says further the above-mentioned puma is a shy and easily frightened animal that attacks flocks and especially sheep, according to them. But where are these flocks and these sheep in the American Forest? Nobody ever heard of sheep in forests.

And besides if he's so shy and easily frightened as the Zingarelli Dictionary of the Italian Language says, why does he attack flocks? I wouldn't want to meet him face to face.

There's also a drawing at the bottom of the page and judging by it, a puma resembles a tiger or a panther. Then don't try to tell me he's shy or easily frightened. You gave yourselves away with this drawing you tried to pass him off as a rabbit but instead

HE'S A FEROCIOUS BEAST.

There are plenty of them in the American Forest, nobody knows what to do about them. Whether to go ahead or to turn back. You have to be very careful because the tawny-colored puma blends with the leaves of the American palm. You can't see him and you don't hear any sound. You're walking along calmly and suddenly he's on you. Like all felines he's a great jumper. He may be as shy and easily frightened as the Zingarelli Dictionary of the Italian Language says, but

HE'S CARNIVOROUS,

if you please.

I'll keep my finger on the trigger of the rifle and you follow me on tiptoe. You look to the right and I'll look to the left. These palm trees with their sharp-edged leaves. This stifling heat. This terrain covered with ferns. These distant roars. These birds that fly off all of a sudden. You can't see the Heavens with all this foliage. It's enough to frighten you. Rosalia looks at me frightened and says what are the two of us doing here in the American Forest? Why don't we go back home, nobody is forcing us to stay. You're right, I said, let's go back to Italy. You leave pumas alone, she said, leave them where they are, in the American Forest.

The police are still searching in the meadow, in the grass, this is no joking matter, Rosmunda said, the police. Once they found in a dead man's eye a portrait of the murderer at the very moment of the crime. And so what? I let out a laugh. Go ahead, she said, laugh, however be careful and don't let them hear you. Remember that

THE POLICE HAVE VERY SHARP EARS,

remember that the ears of the police are terrific, they're better than radar. The police, I said, I can hear better than they can. Do you hear the sirens then? No now I can't hear anything. I realize you can't hear them, you don't want to hear them.

It's the police who are coming their panther-jeeps, she said, in a little while they'll knock at the door and want to come in. Let's pretend it's nothing there's nobody home. If they want to come in, she said, they come in, the police bash down doors like nothing at all, they have a special system I mean they don't bother with the keyhole, they take a crowbar to the hinges. All right, I said, a crowbar if they come in they come in we'll let them come in we have an alibi now anyway.

I sat down to wait, I smoke a cigarette. I think of the condemned man's last cigarette, of the owls circling over the Plain as owls do when they start circling, of the old men sitting on park benches provided there is a park and provided the park has benches. Otherwise they have to sit on the ground and if

[84]

there's grass, on the grass. I don't sit on the ground, much less on the grass.

And now what's happening? Who is doing that shooting? What do they want what do you want? Who are you angry with? I'm ready to swear an oath, tell me what I have to swear and I'll swear it. But let me go.

There in the middle of the meadow they've put up a billboard that says Milkatex, don't tell me you've started exploiting even the dead now with your advertising?

15.

Sunday is a day to spend in the house I go about on my bicycle. In winter I can sit beside the stove and in summer at the window with a book in my hand, I open the door and I go off. Read a book or a picture magazine, collect your thoughts or else open the Bible at random and read a page it always teaches you something. I pedal instead under the Sun or the rain for the whole day. I run about the Planet free and solitary as a rhinoceros.

To the right and left of the road there are oleander bushes with red and pink flowers. Beyond the bushes there are olive trees some pines an arbutus hedge two ancient ilexes a plowed field two rows of vines a meadow. All right maybe I've exaggerated, there isn't everything I said but almost. I push my bicycle up the hill, I'm coming from Casale Abbruciato and I'm returning to Albano.

On the right there is a house built halfway and then abandoned, obviously they changed their minds. Still the place is beautiful the view. There is also a pile of little tufa blocks, there are others of brick and of pozzolana but I can't see any masons there aren't any. There's a cement mixer a length of fencing a roll of barbed wire some pieces of travertine a rusty bicycle. I go closer. The bicycle's the same brand as mine that I'm wheeling along, the same shape and the same color, even the bell is the same and the headlight but this one is a wreck. I look at it carefully, there's a dent in the crossbar of the frame just like mine, exactly the same. It would be mine if I weren't holding mine by my hand. This symmetry. The mud guard is broken whereas mine is barely crumpled. Months or years have gone by since it was abandoned.

I look around and there's nobody but I feel myself being watched. These flowering bushes there's a man hidden behind which. He's pointing his rifle, he's aiming at my forehead, if you please.

THIS SITUATION KEEPS REPEATING ITSELF.

I already feel the bullet hole here to the left under my hairline. He still can't make up his mind to shoot. I expect the shot any minute, I stand here and I don't move. However if I die now it's a disaster, the story will finish ahead of time. Giuseppe, dear friend, you know it isn't true, there are people waiting in line to take your place.

I cover the wreck of the bicycle with some boughs, nobody must see it. I straighten up and go back to the road. I act as if nothing had happened all the same this rusty bicycle. This unfinished house, these oleander bushes. There he's fired but the shot wasn't heard. Not even the whistle of the bullet. Usually bullets whistle when they fly through the air, then they are lost and fall spent to the Earth, your so-called stray bullets. They can be found at any moment, when you're walking along the road or in the middle of a meadow. This one must have fallen very far away, in a meadow or perhaps on the roof of a house or in a canal. It must have fallen some place because lead falls at a certain point. It doesn't fly on its own energy but only through the initial thrust of the gunpowder.

If the bullet had hit me I wouldn't be here to tell the tale, I'd be stretched out on the Earth, I'd already be on my way to the Eternal Cold, if you please. Instead, I'm still on my feet, I am making my way towards Albano. I can think and talk but

IT'S A MIRACLE I'M ALIVE

it's a miracle you're alive, Giuseppe.

Maybe the wind deflected the bullet during its trajectory or maybe he didn't aim carefully. Luckily a man is a very narrow target, as Sergeant Rowan of the U.S. Army says. Between twelve and fifteen inches wide to be precise, you have to be a fairly good shot. It depends on the distance, because at close range anybody can hit the target. There are people however who can't hit the target even at close range, there are people who simply don't know how to hold a rifle if it's a question of a rifle or a revolver if it's a question of a revolver. But maybe it was the wind that saved me. On the contrary the air is as steady as a rock, not a leaf is stirring on the branches. So he aimed badly.

[88]

Since they can't take me alive they are trying to kill me or have me killed. I mean they have paid killers. Somebody would be happier if you were dead, lying on a meadow with your mouth in the grass, Giuseppe. Otherwise why would they have tried to kill you? So don't roam around on the roads only people who have nothing to fear do that. You'd be better off if you dropped out of circulation even if it means going underground the way ants do and certain other animals I don't want to name.

Instead you spend your days roaming the roads having yourself shot at by strangers. You neglect your business, there was a time when you came back to Albano loaded with zinc lead copper brass et cetera et ceterola. If buyers come what kind of businessman are you going to look like are we going to look like? You go roaming about with your bicycle and one day you'll come back with a hole in your head in other words you'll be found dead in the middle of the road. Narrow as you may be a bullet can still hit you in the forehead any minute.

AND AFTERWARDS DON'T COME COMPLAINING.

The mystery of the rusty bicycle. It must be a signal, but who from? Who wants to frighten me? I push my bicycle with an effort up the hill towards Albano, my legs are heavy while I walk but my head is light I feel it flying away.

Beyond the gulley there's a field of potatoes, lucky the man who planted them. I like the Earth cultivated by man. At a certain point he comes to gather the fruit of his labor, lucky man, the peasant who planted the potatoes. There are people instead who stand there with an aimed gun, perhaps as I look calmly around the field of potatoes, he is hidden there behind the hedge and is taking aim to shoot once more. But what hedge? I don't see any hedges around here. It isn't the hedge that counts but the murderer who's hidden behind it.

All right the murderer, but who told him I had to go by here,

WHO WAS THE INFORMER?

There's somebody around here who ought to be on my side but is on his side instead, if you please. He dogs my tracks, sometimes I can feel his breath on my neck it's slippery as a worm's. I'd start yelling but there isn't a living soul around here, they've all hidden they've run off. Where are they, where are you? You hide and then I'll run off too before it becomes completely dark.

It's seven-thirty in the afternoon towards evening, the Sun in a little while has set, against the Heavens the lights of Rome are reflected, a diffused brightness almost violet. It's the lights of the automobiles that run back and forth on the streets with their lights blazing, the neon signs, the spotlights in the Forum and those in the Colosseum. The big bulb in front of the Railroad Station is also turned on it's the most powerful in the World as the guidebooks of the Capital say.

By now I'm near Albano. When I reach my storeroom I'll go inside quickly and I'll slam the door shut behind me. I'll go to sleep. I want to sleep for a whole year without waking up, let me sleep. There are too many people out hunting me you'd think I was a herd of wild game. If you really want to kill me

[90]

kill me in my sleep then I won't even notice it and I'll believe I'm going on sleeping. Amen, like a Christian prayer.

There I'm almost home, I walk on tiptoe. I'm curious now to know how it'll end. Only a few yards to the door of my storeroom. Badly, Rossella says, I'm afraid it ends badly.

16.

The lady of the villa said why what is the Necrophila Funeraria doing around my house? And I said, I mean the fly-killer said, there must be a corpse nearby. That's impossible, the lady of the villa said,

THERE ARE NO CORPSES AROUND HERE.

See here, madam, I said, the Necrophila Funeraria doesn't make mistakes, if there isn't a corpse in the house there must be one in the meadow behind that hedge. And she said what hedge are you talking about, there's nothing behind there I mean there are only weeds and wild shrubs, that is uncultivated fields, it's a place where nobody ever goes. There's a fence of barbed wire all around it.

Nobody has died in this house for years and years there are

no corpses around. My husband died far from here in East Africa in Abyssinia in 1936, during the Abyssinian war. He was advancing with a patrol in the middle of the African Jungle, they mistook him for an Abyssinian and they shot him, the Italians. The lady was crying. The criminals, she said, to mistake him for an Abyssinian. They sent me a telegram with apologies signed by Badoglio.

There must be at least a dead dog or a horse or some other dead animal, I said, I mean Giuseppe the fly-killer said. There are no dogs and there are no horses that go around dying in the fields, she said, if a horse were missing I would have noticed it but it's years since I kept horses and dogs in this house.

If it isn't a dog and if it isn't a horse you'll see madam that it must be a man he can easily have climbed over a barbed wire fence. And she said he must be a strange sort of man to go and die in the middle of a meadow. Why no not at all, I said, dying is the most natural thing there is, it can happen to anybody. I tell you madam that

YOU CAN DIE FOR A TRIFLE.

No, she said, the Necrophila Funeraria has really made a mistake. There are no corpses around here, I'm sure.

If there isn't one today there'll be one tomorrow, I said I mean Giuseppe said, the Necrophila Funeraria has an incredible nose, it smells the odor of corpse even a week before. Keep talking Giuseppe, you're talking about a dead man with that lady.

But then this Necrophila Funeraria is much better than the

police, the police have never arrived a week early on the scene of the crime but more likely a week late. From this point of view you have to take your hat off to the Necrophila Funeraria. However there's this difference, I said to Giuseppe, the police go around hunting for the murderer while the Necrophila Funeraria finds only the victim, if you please. And he said sometimes the police don't find even that.

But then, I said, how did it all end in the villa, with that lady? The flies hadn't made a mistake, Giuseppe says. Cripes you keep talking don't stop. And he said I took a walk around the fields and I found some blood on the Earth near a hut, and there was an old man lying dead in the grass, I said. One moment, Giuseppe said, there was no old man there was only this straw hut. All right a straw hut, I said, where are there any straw huts around this neighborhood? If you ask me you didn't see clearly. In the Stone Age when men were savages, there were huts. We surely haven't gone back a hundred thousand years, by any chance, to the time when there were huts on piles and swamps all around full of crocodiles. If you take a step they eat your leg. And afterwards how will you manage to walk? Life is hard in the midst of these swamps with these crocodiles. There are also gigantic mosquitoes and certain ravenous birds of prey that pluck out your eye with one peck. But what am I doing here alone a hundred thousand years ago, in the midst of crocodiles and mosquitoes and ravenous birds?

The butcher had been there to do some illegal butchering, Giuseppe said, he does what he pleases. Then, I said, it isn't a question of a crime,

IT WASN'T HUMAN BLOOD.

It must have been calves, he said, or other animals for butchering, for the butcher. What does human blood have to do with it?

Giuseppe, dear friend, the fly-killer said they were calves or other animals for butchering, you're wasting your time with him. All right I'm wasting my time I'll waste what I like, if you please.

17.

They say he was wandering around the Pavona Plain and frightening little girls. There are these old men who amuse themselves by frightening little girls, they hide behind a bush and then they jump out all of a sudden with one bound, they make noises with their mouth, gestures. Sometimes the undersigned also does it when he doesn't know what else to do. Partly out of vice and partly for fun, maybe more for fun than out of vice. Also vice however.

They say that he was collecting waste paper, books newspapers and other waste paper. They had seen him pushing a bicycle with a sack on it full of old paper. Nobody looked inside so how can they say it was old waste paper? How can you say it was old waste paper?

THERE COULD HAVE BEEN ANYTHING
INSIDE THAT SACK.

They saw him walking alone on the beach at Torvaianica at night, so they say I mean one woman says so, the wife of the butcher of Pavona. Every now and then he stopped and pricked up his ears to listen to the sound of the sea as if special messages were coming to him from the sea. But we know that only the sound of the waves comes from the sea, especially at Torvaianica. What messages can come from the sea at Torvaianica? This is no joking matter.

He walked barefoot, he stopped to listen and then he began walking again on the beach barefoot with his ears alert for those messages, but what messages? And what was the wife of the butcher of Pavona doing on the beach of Torvaianica at night? What does her husband have to say about that? We should hear him, the butcher, on the subject of what his wife was doing on the beach at Torvaianica at night.

They say the man walking on the beach was a professor disguised as a beggar. One of those professors who go around looking for Roman ruins. They keep hoping to find the Colosseum but often they never find anything. If they find a stone they take it home and show it to their wife. The old man could be one of those professors.

But what was he hoping to find in the Pavona Plain? All right there are some remains of Roman villas it's poor stuff. The rich didn't come here to build villas, in the Plain. So forget the notion of finding treasures, they were poor little houses, you can see that very well from the walls that still remain. You'll never find a marble column, if you want to find

[97]

one you'll have to bring it here like Benito Mussolini did in Piazza Argentina, that costs a lot of money. In general these professors haven't a cent. Then go hunt somewhere else, here you're wasting your time.

He could have been a thief. But a thief of what? There are the so-called chicken thieves but now there isn't any profit in stealing chickens, what with all these chicken factories prices have fallen very low. There are thieves who specialize in automobiles and there are others who don't want to hear automobiles mentioned and they steal only what's inside automobiles, cameras overcoats binoculars gramophones gloves leather purses full or empty. And then there are those who steal according to the occasion and these would be the so-called occasional thieves like gypsies who steal everything on all occasions.

However he wasn't a gypsy, if you please. Unless he was a gypsy disguised as a beggar but the gypsies are all beggars they don't need any disguises. It's happened more than once however that a person goes around dressed like a beggar and then they discover he's a millionaire, when he dies. There are certain millionaires who amuse themselves by playing beggar. In this case

WHERE ARE THE MILLIONS?

Where can he have put them? Did he make a will or, if there's no will and there are no heirs, who gets the millions, the Government? Or the City of Albano? Why don't they divide them a bit all around, millions come in handy for everybody. Even divided by a thousand a million is always a thousand.

[98]

There are also very elegant thieves, like the ones who stay in de luxe hotels and they would be the so-called hotel rats. They speak three or four languages, they drive up in an Alfa Romeo sports car. That old man however didn't have an Alfa Romeo sports car and even if he had one he wasn't a hotel rat, there are no hotels around here and the rats have all run off what with these poisons they've spread around the countryside. Giuseppe, dear friend, soon there will be hotels as Rome gradually stretches towards the sea. All right let Rome stretch towards the sea it would be better off if it stayed where it is.

In any case dressed as badly as he was they wouldn't even let him in so he couldn't steal. In fact

THEY FOUND HIM WITH HIS POCKETS EMPTY.

Then what kind of thief was he? Strange a thief with empty pockets. Giuseppe, dear friend, there are even thieves who have never stolen. They are the most dangerous ones because it's hard to recognize them and they aren't in the police files, so the police themselves don't know how to put them in prison when they run across them. In certain cases they beat them a bit to make them confess.

They say he was a spy, but who for? There's not much to spy on here in the Pavona Plain. There might be the so-called industrial espionage but for that you have to go towards Latina where the factories are that sprang up in the Period of the Boom. Here there's nothing, only chicken farms I mean there aren't even them any more because almost all of them have gone out of business, if you please.

On the other hand if he was a military spy he should have gone to the military airport at Pratica di Mare where the jets are. There aren't any military secrets around Pavona there's an abandoned powder magazine between Ariccia and Genzano it doesn't interest anybody. Then why did he come here to carry out military espionage?

The police have questioned people trying to find somebody who knew him. The daughter of the Pavona tobacconist says I was going out for a ride on my Vespa. I saw an old man who was pedaling along on a black bicycle he was having a hard time pedaling. The road was uphill at eight in the evening towards Albano. Then the old man gets off the bicycle and starts pushing it by hand. He stops to look at a house under construction, to rummage in some wreckage. He was badly dressed. He didn't have eyeglasses but he seemed to have them. I can't say anything else, I'm not sure it was him I mean I might be completely mistaken.

As far as what she says goes the daughter of the Pavona tobacconist might as well have kept her mouth shut.

WHEN IT COMES TO SEEING AN OLD MAN ON A BICYCLE ANYBODY CAN SEE ONE.

People say the murderer, if there is one, at a certain point falls into the net. The net would be the police's. All right the net, but the police make too much noise and the fish is frightened away. Then they sit there and look stupid, they sit and wait, they have plenty of time to wait for the fish in other

words the murderer. The fish is sly, when he sees the net he
runs off in the other direction, the murderer. They are right to
run off both of them, I mean we're back where we started
from, if you please.

18.

How wonderful, Rosalma said, we're all alone you and me in this room. She had shut the door and the window and now that you've shut the door and the window, I said, what are we going to do here in the dark the two of us? Nothing we're going to do nothing but if you like we can even start shouting at the top of our lungs after all nobody can see us here. All right, I said, shouting at the top of our lungs is all well and good but I have to suck I can't shout.

I didn't make myself clear, she said, I mean we can do whatever we like why do you want to start shouting then? Let's invent something, she said, some game to play in a room in the dark. I've had the mattress restuffed, for example. What do you mean you've had the mattress restuffed for example? Rosetta looked at me you can skip the looking at me, I said, you can't see anything in the dark anyway. Even on the ground I mean on the floor, she said, we could play some game. Let's think it over for a moment, I said, there's not much to invent in the way of a game, we can watch Television if you like. I watch it by myself whenever I please.

And with all your imagination, she said. Let me think what can be done in the dark something two can play, I said, there's this thing I used to do in the fifth grade. Then you don't understand, she said,

A CHILD'S GAME.

Not all that much of a child's game, the Chinese do it too they're expert at these games. If you don't mind explaining, she said, all right I'll explain now you have to do what I tell you let's see what you tell me.

It's very simple, I said, you just sit down there with your eyes wide open. Listen, with my eyes wide open or not you'd better tell me what I'm supposed to look at in complete darkness there's nothing to see. It isn't a matter of looking and she said I don't like jokes at a time like this. All right, you don't like jokes it isn't a joke it's a Chinese erotic game. I don't know if I'm going to like this game or not, I sit here on this chair and then what do you do? It's very simple, I said, I sit here too and

I LICK YOUR EYE.

You lick my eye? Yes, I lick it with my tongue and you let it be licked. I don't know if I understand or not, you want to lick my eye, this is supposed to be fun? She sat on the chair and she was looking at me with her eyes wide. There's nothing to look at.

Better not the eye, she said. You'll see you just have to begin it's like with everything else and she said let's wait a moment, I'm afraid it'll hurt me. At the beginning no games are fun, maybe the first time it'll hurt you a little but afterwards you'll like it wait and see, come on let me lick it.

I would like to know, she said, just who has the fun the one who licks or the one who is licked. What kind of question is that, they are different pleasures like when a man and a woman do it together. I understand all that but this isn't the same I mean I can lick or be licked and vice versa both you and I have tongues and eyes, in other words.

All right we both have tongues and eyes these explanations, I said, I remember only that it was a lot of fun in the fifth grade with this girl cousin of mine. You had a cousin yes I had one there's nothing wrong with that, a girl cousin. Well well this cousin, she said, this is the first I've heard of her. You can't be jealous retroactively now we're going to have

JEALOUSY.

I had barely begun with the tip of my tongue. Easy, she said, take it easy you're hurting me, easy easy I like it. There that's it go slowly, she said, I see all these flowers, now you're hurting me. Of course I'm hurting you but pleasure is also included in the pain. The eye is connected with the brain and the spinal fluid, I said, it transmits a shock to the whole body, it's like touching the wires of the Industrial Current you think you're going to be electrocuted by which. That's true, I feel

[104]

myself trembling all over, I'm trembling from head to foot, I see so many flowers of every color.

There, she said, a little harder that's right I like it. I believe Napoleon liked it too. This is no joking matter, I don't know about Napoleon, this great lover. But did he lick or was he licked? I believe he was licked, so I have heard. Now a little bit harder, she said, try moving your tongue around and I'll follow you with my eye in a circular direction, there like that, move faster, like a wheel.

All these flowers. I see a celestial meadow of many colors the sea all purple and orange a wheel that turns a butterfly a canary. A gold fruitcake twenty-four karats a pastry dove, as if it were Easter and Christmas together. I see a pink cloud and a bell that's ringing, how many things you see Rosa dear in this room that's dark as a cellar. I see them with my mind, she said, but what about you I don't understand how you can talk when your tongue is busy licking. It's true, how can I manage to talk, if you please?

I had stopped for a moment to smoke. Throw that cigarette away it's bad for you, she said, how marvelous now we can lock ourselves in and we'll only go out to buy food once a week. She had both eyes open wide. Let me finish this cigarette hurry up all right I'll hurry now let me smoke.

At the start, I said, you mustn't overdo. Remember that

THE EYE IS VERY DELICATE.

You know it can be worn out by licking? And what about the Chinese, she said, and Napoleon then? In fact the Chinese over the centuries have worn out their eyes, if you've noticed they have smaller eyes than normal. I don't believe it, she said, she was laughing to split her sides. Laugh laugh, I said, split your sides. There's nothing to laugh about, the Chinese.

She was all sweating and trembling. Again, she said, just five minutes or so and then we'll stop. And I said it's best for us to wait till tomorrow, the game is more beautiful when you develop a yearning for it otherwise if you play it continually what, she said, you can't leave me halfway, can't you see I'm trembling? In fact she was trembling.

Her eye was weeping, it had reddened a little. It's nothing, she said, I haven't got used to it yet, just five minutes and then we'll stop. Look if I want to I can eat it in one mouthful, I was joking luckily, not joking all that much. You want to frighten me, she said, you don't frighten me, you're a barking dog that doesn't bite. Watch out for certain dogs that bark and then jump on you all of a sudden and tear off an arm or a leg with one bite. Dobermanns for example are treacherous dogs, they even bite their master and also his friends and relatives, if you please. They say dogs are loyal to man, not all that loyal. In certain cases dogs have torn man limb from limb.

19.

I see a black meadow and a green bird the High Tension wires the Sun on one side and the Moon on the other the transparent air and the flight of a bumblebee a white cloud shaped like a horse and an Alitalia Caravelle with its distant rumble. Out of the corner of one eye I also see the Mediaeval Tower. The Caravelle disappears in the direction of the sea, it's left a strange vibration in the air which mingles with that of the Santa Palomba tower of the Italian Radio. Back and forth on the meadow a dog's paws, I see many human legs too, civilian and military, people's voices talking. Keep talking,

IN THE END YOU WON'T HAVE ANYTHING
LEFT TO SAY.

The ants give me no peace, you can't have a moment's quiet. A blade of grass penetrates one of my ears a rock hurts my back the flies walk around on my face on my nose on my lips on my eyes. The Sun scorches my skin, my eyes are about to burst. I feel little stings, is it the flies or the ants? Someone is touching me why are you touching me?

I see two ravens flying very high in the Heavens. They are black. They circle around and make their raven sounds. What have they come to this neighborhood for? What do they think they'll find, what do you think you'll find? Go away go somewhere else, there's nothing for you here.

Why don't you cover me? You must have a sheet. If you don't have one you can buy it in a shop here in Pavona or in Albano, a sheet doesn't cost much. You don't leave a human being like this a prey to the flies with ravens circling in the Heavens. If you can't find a sheet put a blanket over me you must have one, even a handkerchief over my face is better than nothing.

I would like to stand up a while I'm tired, you don't get tired only from walking. I'd like to stretch my legs and then go sit in the shade of a tree and smoke a French cigarette in peace. Nobody helps me stand up naturally why don't you help me? Help him stand up, give him a hand.

There I've found the shade of a tree but what became of the tree where has it gone? It seems to be the shade of a stone pine. Giuseppe, dear friend, whether it's an ilex or a stone pine what's the difference? Be content with the shade, what does the tree matter to you?

They are still talking about me, their words become interwoven, they form transparent geometries in the transparent air. I must move, talk to somebody, but I don't know who.

[108]

IS THERE SOMEBODY WHO WANTS TO
TALK WITH ME?

I can even talk to myself, if I like, however if I find somebody else it's better. We will sit in the shade and chat a little and smoke a cigarette apiece. Isn't there anybody who wants to talk with me? I also need to stretch my lungs. I don't know why, but I can't breathe here. Help me breathe, there's plenty of air around here, you don't want it all for yourselves, I hope.

Then there's simply nobody who wants to talk with me? I would like to know so many things, I'm dying to know them. Who is that old man I mean who was he, what kind of life did he lead when I was alive. What did I do when you were alive. I have some terrible suspicions, if you please. I have to talk about it with somebody, quickly.

I can make a phone call but I don't have anybody to phone and even if I phoned him I don't know if he could answer my questions. A try wouldn't hurt. But can I just start talking with the first person who comes along? That depends, I'd have to see what sort he is. There are people that when you talk to them for the first time you feel you've known them a hundred years. So I say hello, can we talk? And he says go ahead, Giuseppe, I'm listening. He calls me by my first name right away as if he too had known me a hundred years.

I'd like to talk to somebody like that, I'd almost be willing to telephone him. But I don't have the number and I can't even look it up in the directory because I don't know what his name is. What do you care about knowing his name anyway? Call him all the same. And then I'll say hello who am I speaking with? And he says this is Giuseppe speaking.

CRIPES, ANOTHER GIUSEPPE.

My God how many of us are there? I hang up in a hurry and then I call up a woman, she can't be named Giuseppe. But will she know how to answer my questions? We'll see.

Maybe she hasn't even read the newspaper and then I'll have to tell the whole story from the beginning to the end what a bore. I must be careful not to let something compromising slip out, there's the risk that she might run straight to the police. It's easy enough to end up in Regina Coeli, the work of a moment. Just a word too much or too little.

Am I wise to run this risk? Just for the pleasure of hearing her warm voice, provided she has a warm voice because if her voice is cold and shrill it's useless, I won't run any risks for a woman who has a cold and shrill voice. Especially when I don't know her. However she calls me by my first name, she says don't worry Giuseppe I won't say anything to anybody. All right you won't say anything to anybody and I thank you, however see here there's not much to say, I'm innocent. This doesn't mean a thing, she says, there are many types of innocent people, there are some innocent people who deserve twenty years in jail.

Just a minute, twenty years in jail! Speak out, whose side are you on, mine or the police's? And she says don't worry you can confide in me you've found a friend.

Giuseppe, dearest friend, watch out for this woman, you met her by chance in the Albano telephone directory, in other words a chance meeting, don't talk with her. But who shall I talk with then? You can talk with me freely, she said, you were lucky to meet me. Thank goodness, I said, I was lucky. And she said luckily luck also exists, otherwise the famous brick could fall on your head while you're walking along the sidewalk.

Who said anything about a brick on the head? I don't want to hear that brick mentioned. And this buzz, what is it? Talk louder I can't hear anything. Silence, the conversation is already finished.

But why am I here? Something's gone wrong. But what's wrong? See here I'm not sleepy I don't want to sleep, you go to sleep yourselves if you're sleepy. Sleep talk take pictures pray telephone do what you like, I'm tired of these arms of these legs of this head, I want to get up and walk. I want to move too I can't stay here immobile forever waiting for what?

20.

I see in the distance the roofs the towers and the plate glass of the factories that sprang up in the Period of the Boom. I've heard that they intend building others with the help of the Southern Italy Development Fund and then skyscrapers for the people who work there, in other words little by little

A METROPOLIS

much bigger than Rome and Milan put together.

Somebody is already working to build this great Metropolis without knowing it. Look at a map. These roads drawn in parallel lines according to the Italian Grid will be the great arterial roads of tomorrow. Is there a Secret Mind at work on this project or does it grow by itself like a thing in nature? I wonder.

From the air you can already see the pattern of the Metropolis but nobody is aware of it. Or did Captain Giudicini become aware of something when he made his General Survey? Or is this why all those balloons went up with the ballooners and the cameramen? What became of them? You can't see them any more nobody talks about them, they've disappeared into the Heavens.

At a certain point you open your eyes and the Metropolis is all built and you say why look at all the skyscrapers, look at all the automobiles, how they rush around. Barely a hundred years have gone by how they rush too, the years. What are a hundred years? Nothing, a hundred years pass in a minute, they go by and you aren't even aware of it.

Forget the anthill trauma, the architects said that is they say so today. All right forget the anthill trauma but what do you think you've made with your skyscrapers of reinforced concrete, steel copper stainless aluminum and other stainless metals? Haven't you actually constructed an anthill or what would you call it?

Where the Mediaeval Tower used to be there is a Huge General Market that covers the whole meadow. In the middle there is a plaza of pebbled metal you can't slip on which. The signs are copper you can't erase. But there are too many automobiles that run back and forth in the streets they make a continuous rumble which causes the houses to shake I mean the skyscrapers, with all their steel and reinforced concrete. Naturally the air is seriously polluted

I HAVE A HARD TIME BREATHING.

But why, I ask you, don't they put electric automobiles into circulation seeing that they've already invented them? Otherwise what did you invent them for? They tell me that the Great Petroleum Trusts don't want it. So the air is full of carbon monoxide and you can breathe only on the top floors of the skyscrapers. Down in the streets of the Metropolis the air is poisoned and I say steps must absolutely be taken, what do you intend doing? The carbon monoxide lies stagnant in the streets, it enters the shops the houses, through the elevator shafts it reaches even the top floors and it poisons one and all.

YOU CAN'T BREATHE AROUND HERE.

It's scandalous that in such a modern city they haven't found a system for keeping the atmosphere clean. What do they need? If you can't use electric automobiles go on bicycles or else shut off the exhaust pipes. The carbon monoxide comes from them, that is from the exhaust pipe of the engine. That's where the noise comes from. If you don't want to close off the exhaust pipes find another method of getting from place to place.

I follow an elementary line of reasoning and I say gentlemen have you built sewers to take away the refuse of the Metropolis? Then build great pipes to carry off the polluted air. Then make more pipes to bring clean air into the city, mountain air and sea air according to whether a person prefers mountain air or sea air. You can link up directly with San Remo for those who want San Remo air, with Cortina and the Val d'Aosta for those who want Cortina and the Val d'Aosta air. Don't you import fruit from Africa? Then import air from where the air is good and clean because here the air is a mess. It doesn't cost anything, air exists in abundance, if you please. There's only the expense of the pipe installation to amortise.

It's pointless to say once upon a time there was a meadow here there was a hedge here there was the Mediaeval Tower here the Fosso dei Preti and here Casale Abbruciato. In fact nobody says this and nobody remembers any more what was here before, a hundred years have gone by maybe two hundred, even the maps of the Military Topographical Institute have disappeared. You can't die any longer in the middle of a meadow because there aren't any meadows, nobody can fall with his mouth in the grass because you can't find any grass.

When they walk along the street the people hold their breath, if they have some sorrow they can't sigh, if they're irritated they can't snort. They can't even talk for fear of dying of poison. They don't look one another in the eye because they all wear glasses with those reflecting lenses that let you look but you can't be looked at. They all go around with revolvers in their pockets, special small revolvers as thin as a sheet of paper. Pointless crimes are committed and nobody pays any attention. They've abolished Christmas Easter and New Year's, they've changed the whole calendar.

Change the air instead of the calendar and you'll be better off. You can't breathe around here I feel I'm suffocating, if you please. How do you manage?

DO YOU HAVE LUNGS?

Or do you breathe with your feet what do you breathe with? Maybe with your skin in general. Or are you like fish that have a special system for breathing? I protest. But it's useless to protest, the authorities won't do a thing. You have to put up with them because they are still in the future otherwise a massacre would be in order.

However the blame is also yours, I mean every citizen's. The street on which you walk the house in which you live the office in which you are employed the automobile in which you rush the shoes and the clothes you wear whatever place you occupy whatever the hour or the season I want to see you sink out of sight along with the street on which the house in which the office where the automobile in which the shoes the clothes whatever the place whatever the hour and the season, et cetera et ceterola.

There are no more mice squirrels lizards crickets cicadas as there were once upon a time, in the Pavona Plain. Because the Pavona Plain no longer exists now there's the Metropolis. There are no more flies and ants. If there were they'd die of starvation. The doors and the windows are shut hermetically and they can't get into the houses, there's nothing around to eat. Even the cockroaches that eat dung have died of starvation.

To make up for it there are plenty of human beings, the Metropolis is overpopulated, that's why so many crimes take place every day and nobody says anything. It isn't like the old days, I mean like now, when they leave a dead man in the middle of a meadow. A man doesn't even have time to draw breath but what he's carried off by a firm of specialists and he ends up in the sewers that lead to the sea. For that matter, I address the citizens, you have what you deserve. You'll end up being murdered all of you, you'll murder one another like ravening wolves.

Or else asphyxiated. Look at your faces. You're all sick, you're ugly in form and color.

YOU LOOK HORRIBLE.

Carbon monoxide is like D.D.T. and you breathe it from morning till night. I told you how it'll all end you'll all sink from view, along with the streets on which you walk the house in which you live the office in which you're employed the automobile in which you rush

SO MUCH THE WORSE FOR YOU.

Rosalinda says don't get angry about this Metropolis before it exists, don't quarrel with the citizens who aren't born yet. All right I won't quarrel with the citizens but can you smell the carbon monoxide that comes in and you can't breathe? And this constant buzz where does it come from? Where do these vapors come from? They come from the Metropolis well let them come. But I say my anger is all directed towards the future. See here the future is very far away, Rosina says, you have a long time to wait. Not all that long, the future comes quickly enough, maybe while you're there waiting for it the future has already come and a minute later it's already gone by.

21.

It wasn't a black dog it was a man with a cap on his head. The police have questioned Giuseppe the fly-killer they were right to question him. Then who was this character and he says it was the beach attendant at the Seaview Baths at the Lido di Lavinio however I may be wrong. You may be wrong, try not to be and you'll be better off.

Thanks, Giuseppe says, I don't wear a cap on my head and I don't have a black bicycle. I saw him going along the Santa Maria in Fornarola road towards the Mediaeval Tower, that is if you saw him go by you were also going along that road with your black bicycle, the police say. Yes, I was going by but so was he, the beach attendant, says Giuseppe, what is a beach attendant doing on a bicycle in the evening in the midst of the Pavona Plain? His place is on the beach of the Seaview Baths or else in a boat or a raft in the midst of the sea.

Go on, track down this beach attendant,

ARREST HIM IMMEDIATELY.

Why don't you arrest him? There's no sea there's no beach there are no boats here for a beach attendant. There isn't even a river around these parts, there are meadows but they never have time to become green before the Sun burns everything up, that is the grass. What the Sun doesn't burn the peasants burn in summer, the stubble along the road. Wouldn't it be better to cut it with a scythe? Or are you afraid of hurting your fingers? You've burned down century-old trees with your fires along the edge of the roads, one of these days you'll burn yourselves up too with your shoes hat and all the clothes you have on, if you please. What are the Forest Rangers doing? If there's a law see that it is obeyed and if there isn't one see that it is obeyed anyway.

Giuseppe goes on to say this character with the black bicycle, this beach attendant from the Seaview Baths of Lido di Lavinio that I saw going by at night in the vicinity of the Mediaeval Tower, on the other hand I believe I may have made a mistake. Maybe he's a fisherman from Anzio. All right, I say, let's suppose he was a fisherman, you can't see what he was doing on a bicycle here in the Plain.

THERE ARE NO FISH AROUND THESE PARTS,

I mean there are fish in the lakes of Nemi and Castel Gandolfo. There are no lakes here, there are only some ditches with polluted water.

There is a river that runs from the lake of Castel Gandolfo all the way to the sea but it's underground. This underground

[119]

river has never been seen by anybody in other words you can't see it but it goes right under the houses of Pavona, if a person puts his ear to the Earth he hears the noise. Naturally in this underground river there are no fish and even if there were they couldn't be caught. So what was that fisherman doing around here then?

There're no two ways about it, to fish you have to go to the lakes or else out to sea which isn't far away. That's where the fish are. The sea is better than the lakes in any case. In the Castel Gandolfo lake there isn't much to fish for any more, all the mullet died nobody knows the reason why. The Fish and Wild Life Department men put them in the lake to restock it and they died. One morning they began rising to the surface bellies up, the current washed them to the shore, the people wanted to eat them. Flocks of birds came down from the Heavens, they also wanted to eat them. The newspapers were full of it.

The woman who runs the Hydrology Laboratory in Rome says the analyses revealed no signs of poisoning or disease. But then what did they die of, according to her? Of old age? Mullet reproduce themselves only in sea water and here they were uncomfortable, the Hydrology Laboratory says. They went around the lake hunting for the sea.

The Laboratory says that in hunting for the sea they forgot to eat and they died of starvation. They thought they would find the sea and instead they found death. The Pescara Ichthyological Center is of the same opinion, in other words they died of starvation because they forgot to eat, I don't believe it.

If you ask me the lake water is polluted and the fish died of poisoning, if you please. It isn't the first time that the Castel

Gandolfo lake has attracted the attention of the newspapers. What did you throw in there? Why did you poison them? I can well believe the mullet died, with that poison. And what does the Public Health Office say? Why doesn't it say anything? Nobody mentions the poison. Not even the police. Then

WATCH OUT I'LL CALL THE CARABINIERI.

In certain cases you have to set up a rivalry between the carabinieri and the police. There is this antagonism between them, you have to feed the flame.

A fisherman who knows his business doesn't come looking for fish here in the Plain, I don't understand why a person would even want to look for fish in these parts. Go away and you'll be better off take your nets with you, go where you like but don't get the idea of catching fish in this place because there are no fish here and there never will be. A fisherman knows these things, this is no joking matter.

So I say beach attendant or fisherman it's the same thing, they shouldn't be riding their bicycle around these parts at night. What are the police waiting for? Why don't they arrest both of them?

22.

On the beach there was a dog barking a child crying a girl singing a wind blowing, the Radio was broadcasting *Helpful Hints for You* on the Second Program. But when you say for you, who do you mean? Who might these you be? Is it me by any chance? Then you're wasting your time, I don't take hints from anybody. And least of all from you Radio people.

There is an old man sitting in a deck chair under a beach umbrella. He's my grandfather, the attendant says, all right your grandfather, he looked like a mummy. I don't like this old man this mummy. I don't like old people in general.

A dead man is nothing, the attendant says, I fish up three or four every year, sometimes it's the sea that tosses them up on the beach. I'm speaking of dead by drowning. He was speaking of dead by drowning, cripes what a nasty job, I said. Nice or nasty I'm the one who's the beach attendant. He had a bicycle, black in form and color. He kept it in the shade under the umbrella. Here we are, I said, here is the murderer.

They saw you at night on your bicycle in the neighborhood of Pavona near the Mediaeval Tower, I said, how can you explain this fact, I mean a beach attendant doesn't go around at night in the Plain what would he go there for? And then I said point-blank to the beach attendant

ARE YOU THE ONE WHO MURDERED HIM?

The beach attendant laughed, laugh laugh there's not much to laugh about. Maybe you've mistaken me for somebody else, he said, all right maybe I'm mistaken let me make a mistake. Not all that mistaken, there are witnesses. The beach attendant spat in the sand, he said a beach attendant can go where he likes, even in Africa if he wants to. Why Africa, I said, why so far away?

In Africa there's the sea, the beach attendant said, and then there are cities and countryside, there are also mountains with snow. All right snow in Africa, but what are you going there for? Are you thinking of running away? You've done something wrong in that case. Be careful, I said, in Africa there are lions and other ravenous beasts. People like to move around, the beach attendant said, there are people who go around the World because they like to travel. What people, I said, who are you talking about? Nothing, I'm talking about That Character who reached Africa across the sea in a boat. And who is he, I said, This Character?

Never mind, he landed in Africa tired and hungry, you know what being tired and hungry means? You mention lions

and ravenous beasts and instead he finds a very nice African
lady,

A QUEEN.

You take a long time to come to the point, I said, cripes how
long he takes to come to the point this beach attendant with
this African queen. All right this queen, I said, but why do
you spit in the sand, you do nothing but spit. This is the place
where you work, the Seaview, even the old man had taken to
spitting. Spit spit, the more you spit.

We'll spit as much as we like, the beach attendant said, all
right but in the meanwhile what is That Character doing? He's
just got to Africa, he said. But why so far off? Nothing, it's
only there you can find an African queen with black skin, that
is That Character could find her. All right with black skin, I
said, like bicycles there are black ones and yellow ones with
yellow skin, in China, and there are also other colors according
to the paint, even with metallic finish and then there are those
with white skin, naturally. The beach attendant said in Africa
they are all black, that is African.

That Character, said the beach attendant, the queen says to
him stay here in my house you can rest. If I want I can give
you a city, you want a city for a present? In Africa, I said, an
African city, naturally. Cripes what a stroke of luck for That
Character. Instead he doesn't want to stay there, I haven't time
I have to go to Italy, he said, that is he wanted to come here to
the Lido di Lavinio right to this beach where we are now
chatting. With all the places there are, I said.

[124]

Don't leave don't abandon me, said the queen, and he said it's no use your insisting

I'M GOING.

You're going don't go, the queen was losing her mind over That Character, like when a woman loses her mind over somebody. Don't leave, she moaned and cried.

Nothing doing, one evening a storm breaks while they're far from home out in the country. All this water down our backs, said the queen, it'll be bad for us. There are no trees to take shelter under, so they take refuge in a cave and here all hell breaks loose, that is they roll on the Earth like two wild creatures. In a cave on the Earth, I said, not bad. Nothing doing, she screamed and tore her hair, said the beach attendant, anyway nobody can see us here, a queen has to be careful not to be seen by her subjects. All right her subjects, I said, I can't wait for That Character to come here to Italy, I want to find out what he's coming for, what he thinks he's going to find.

After what happened in the cave during the storm, the queen says I want to see now if you're staying or going, I want to see what you'll do. Nothing doing, he still wants to leave I have to go, he said, I have a sort of appointment with destiny. All right destiny, I said, but what a strange type This Character is he's behaving like a dog with that queen. She sets up a big wail, the beach attendant says, if you leave I'll kill myself on the spot the very same day, but he didn't believe it those are just things they say. Cripes, I said, couldn't he stay on a few weeks?

Nothing doing, said the beach attendant, at night they all go to sleep including the queen. Then That Character gets out of bed on tiptoe and runs to set sail on a ship and when she wakes up what does she say? The queen doesn't say a word, she has them set fire to a pile of wood and then she throws herself in the midst of the flames in other words she dies by burning herself up. Poor thing I'm sorry, poor woman poor queen burning herself up like that. Oh well, said the beach attendant, she's burned up by now. And what about That Character?

That Character is already at sea and is sailing in the midst of a storm which carries off the helm of the ship and also the helmsman. Cripes things look bad for him if you ask me, I said, let's hope he doesn't sink now with the ship. Does he know how to swim at least? Then, said the beach attendant, That Character takes over command of the sails himself and finally he lands right on this beach where the Seaview Baths are now and from here the story goes on more quickly thank God.

It's funny, though, that This Character liked this Lido di Lavinio there are plenty of places better than which. Rapallo for example. You can see for yourself I said, frankly they're all bare these places, the sea is dirty and the countryside is all burned. I was beginning to yawn, I said why don't you tell me how it ends? Apart from the queen,

IS THERE A DEAD BODY AT THE END?

Tell me more, I said, you said that from here the story goes on more quickly.

Nothing doing, I'll go on if I like, that's enough for now, I said, I'm only interested in that old man when he dies in the middle of the meadow. What old man are you talking about what meadow? For the moment, the beach attendant said, we are still here on the sand. That Character has just landed and in a little while he meets Lavinia who would be the person who gives the name to the Lido di Lavinio. I don't understand, I said, this Lavinia while the Lido here is called Lavinio which would be a man's name. As time goes by, said the beach attendant, they mix up masculine and feminine but these are trifling things. Trifling I wouldn't say, there can be very serious mixups with masculine and feminine and vice versa, if you please.

I'd like to know who this Lavinia is she's the daughter of a king but where are there any kings around these parts? I can't understand, I said, what kind of story you're telling me with all these kings these queens. In those days there were kings and queens all over the place. See here, I said, what days are you talking about? The old man said don't you know about ancient days? Those days.

So, at a certain point those two wanted to get married. What two are you talking about? Aeneas and Lavinia. Finally, I said, somebody who isn't named Giuseppe thank God, this Aeneas. No, said the beach attendant, I'm the one who's named Giuseppe, cripes is that really your name? There's nothing strange about that, he said. All right, I said, I mean all wrong.

Then those two would like to get married, love at first sight. Just a minute, I said, this is a story I've already heard somewhere, it seems to me there's also a book that speaks of which. Don't tell me somebody has written a book without saying anything to us, said the beach attendant, who was it? The old man had become very black, he had taken to spitting again.

There, I said, now I remember this story is called

Thieves, the old man said, then they stole it from us and I said see here it's a famous story that they even read in school. The old man cursed and spat in the sand. The beach attendant had also started spitting.

Giuseppe, my dear friend, I'm sorry but you'd make a dog laugh with these third degrees of yours. You've had somebody tell you the *Aeneid*. I understand I had them tell me the *Aeneid* but at a certain point I realized it. I'm like the police, I follow oblique trails and in this way you'd make a dog laugh. All right I'd make a dog laugh, this voice behind my back, it can happen to anybody to make a dog laugh every now and then.

23.

There's this boy, says Rosalba, I understand there's this boy, I say. He must be seventeen more or less but he could also be twenty or almost. All right, I say, he could also be twenty or almost. I've known this boy since he was born, go ahead I understand, I understand perfectly. That's all, I haven't anything more to say. Very well, I say, then that's all if you haven't anything more to say. Go ahead, silly slut.

This boy brings me mozzarella all right he brings you mozzarella and milk. Milk too but you rush things, you rush your imagination too much. All right I rush my imagination too much, I'm imaginative. You're imaginative, you rush too much you rush your imagination too much.

There's one thing I haven't told you about this boy, a thing you haven't told me, all right. I don't know if I'll tell you, I really don't know. I'm here, I'm in no hurry I can wait you can wait so much the better. I can wait even for years.

Well, says Rossanda, I wanted to tell you that this boy is a boy. All right, this is a very important thing to know this thing that you've said just now if by any chance you have other things to say I'm right here all ears.

Let's go on with this boy all right we'll go on.

THIS BOY IS NAMED GIUSEPPE.

Cripes, I say, he's named Giuseppe too. Where will this all end? By now there are so many of these Giuseppes. So many Giuseppes are no small amount. Wait, the best part is still to come I haven't told you all yet. You haven't told me all yet then go ahead.

This boy is my son. He's your son, I say, that's wonderful. You see you're pleased? Yes I'm pleased, I'm really pleased to know that this boy who's named Giuseppe is your son, but let's hope let's try to hope let's hope what should we hope for?

There's another thing I haven't told you, says Rosangela. Another thing still, I say, all right. Then let's see how I take it. I am really curious to see how you take it, for that matter I'm curious also to see how I take it. Badly, if you ask me you'll take it badly. You can't be sure, on certain days I'm jolly and I take everything with a laugh. Mind you there's nothing to laugh about. Who's laughing?

IS THERE SOMEBODY LAUGHING AROUND HERE?

I'm not laughing there's nothing to laugh about. How do you know there's nothing to laugh about? I can't tell you the answer, I was wrong to think it, this time I was really wrong. You see you were wrong?

This boy who delivers mozzarella and who also delivers your milk from the Central Dairy of Albano. If you had waited a moment I would have told you about the milk, it's no use your running ahead with your words. You're right, if you want I can retrace my steps with my words, the milk from the Central Dairy of Albano. That's better. There, I've retraced my steps. That boy who delivers my mozzarella, Rosella looks at me and then goes ahead, and the Springtime Milk from the Frosinone Milk Products Co. Springtime Milk, I say, why just think of that I thought it was the milk from the Central Dairy in Albano.

All right, that boy is our son. Cripes, I say, I wasn't expecting that. This is really a surprise, a son. And how is he, is he well? And tell me, does he look like me? I'd almost prefer not, the less he looks like me the better. What sort is he? His character I mean. For example is he the angry kind does he become angry easily? I hope he's gone to school regularly, I set great store by education. I don't want an ignorant son like certain sons of certain fathers who don't know the meaning of the word education. This son, a Giuseppe too, cripes I don't know what to say. He's our son, says Rossana, nothing wrong in that.

All right he's our son, I say, but now I want to ask you another question go ahead and ask. Maybe I won't ask you this question that is if he's connected in some way with that old man, you know who I mean. Yes he spoke to me about him, Rosanna says he thought the man was his father. But I'm his father, if you please. And she said I don't know if it's best for you. All right then tell me what I must do. Nothing, do nothing if you want to be calm if I want to be calm, not all that calm.

You haven't told me what type this son is is he a violent type? Have you heard by any chance that he's dead set against his father? And when he delivers the mozzarella and the milk from the Central Dairy in Albano I mean Springtime Milk from the Frosinone Milk Products Co., what do you and Giuseppe do? What do you talk about we talk very little you must say something to each other almost nothing. What do you do? What does the rhinoceros son do with its rhinoceros mother? I don't know what the rhinoceros son does with its rhinoceros mother but I've heard it said that rhinoceroses do it every which way even among close relatives. All right. Not all right at all, I said, all right my foot. All right your foot then, said Roselda.

If you don't talk how can I know what you do? I thought I had told you no you haven't told me anything. Then I'll tell you, we do a bit of everything. A bit of everything? What kind of everything do you do? What the rhinoceros son and the rhinoceros mother do. Explain yourself more clearly, I don't know exactly what the rhinoceros son and the rhinoceros mother do. Well, Rosalia said, if you don't know, I'm not sure I want to explain it to you.

24.

And so it turns,

THE WHEEL OF LIFE.

But what wheel? There is only one wheel of life. Then I don't
like this wheel. I see things as they happen, marching in single
file one after the other but at a certain point they start running
instead, you have to turn somersaults to keep from being run
over by the wheel.

I've discovered I have a son, all of a sudden. She could have
mentioned him before, his mother. She could have said this is
your son and you are his father, I would have said all right
with me it's a fine thing having a son, if you only know it. Not
so fine however if this son goes around looking for his father
in order to murder him. One man's already stretched out in

the meadow covered with ants, the next might be you, if you please.

But what are the police doing then? Why don't they protect me? Instead they're running after me. Rosmunda says see here at a certain point not even the police can spend all their time running, they get tired. And what do all these people want? It seemed there was nobody in the Plain, it looked like a desert waste and then people began popping up on all sides like ants.

Where do these people come from who are popping up on all sides, who go back and forth like ants? Why don't they go home? Watch out, I say, for your life. I'll worry about my life you just watch out for yours. Watch out because anything can happen any moment. Watch out for your life and I'll watch out for mine. Watch out for your life and you'll be better off, watch out for your lives. Just watch out for yours and I'll attend to mine and you others

WATCH OUT FOR YOUR LIVES.

You can't put any faith in what people say often they make up things, they say what comes into their head without thinking about it. Think before you speak instead the opposite happens.

Giuseppe, dear friend, haven't you read the newspapers? All right in the summer the newspapers never know what to say I mean what to write, they sit around idle waiting for something to happen. There aren't many wars and always the same ones, small and far away. The city people are all on vacation at the

[134]

sea and in the mountains, if anybody crops up dead according to the newspapers he was murdered.

I'm tired of walking why don't we sit down on a stone and rest? I mean see here he might have died a natural death. He was walking in the Sun in the meadow, he fainted. Or else he had a weak heart, he had a stroke. You remember the Commodore? He died that way too, because of his heart, and nobody said he was murdered. One can still be hopeful about the past, things might not have gone the way they went. But then what about the blood the knife and the other things found in the meadow?

It's no use your looking at me with suspicion, I say the police may have seen things wrong. Giuseppe, dear friend, this man was killed murdered, the grass was all red you saw yourself the alfalfa flowers stained with blood on the contrary I didn't see anything. There are the color photographs. But why do you want to begin there, with the meadow? You mix up Before with After, begin instead with the murderer not the meadow, and find the proof. At this point the monk from Genzano emerges.

He says he saw a man going by on a bicycle and he had a cigarette in his mouth. It wasn't the beach attendant from the Seaview Baths of the Lido di Lavinio, it was a boy of about eighteen, a young man. There are plenty of young men and a cigarette doesn't mean anything, who doesn't smoke a cigarette every now and then? I also smoke my cigarettes but you're old, you aren't a young man. All the same that monk from Genzano, I said, why is he going in a meadow at night? A monk can go where and when he likes and if he sees a young man on a bicycle he has every right to see him.

They questioned the monk. It was night and the Heavens were serene. If the cigarette was lighted and that young man was motionless against the Starry Heavens, the tip of the cigarette could be mixed up with a Star or a Planet. Come come, Giuseppe, how can anyone mix up a Star or a Planet with the tip of a cigarette? But I tell you all sorts of things are mixed up in this world and sometimes worse even than that.

ONCE A MAN WAS MIXED UP WITH A DOG.

If the man was walking along the road while the Stars were motionless in the Heavens, then the lighted tip could be mixed up with a Comet, the moving fire. Giuseppe, dear friend, even in movement how can you mix up a Comet with the lighted tip of a cigarette? I believe everything, the Universe expanding to Infinity in the Starry Heavens, I believe anything you want, but the tip of a cigarette with a Comet, this is no joking matter. See here they make even worse mix-ups than this, once six million men were mixed up with

SIX MILLION DOGS.

And this is how the wheel of life turns. This young man on a bicycle, this monk from Genzano. Did the monk see his face has he at least given a description of his features? Or is he just talking to hear himself talk this nocturnal monk from Genzano?

Giuseppe, dear friend, sometimes things are mixed-up by nature. All right, nature's mix-ups, you have to go slowly with these mix-ups. Six million men went up in smoke through a mix-up, they were dispersed in the air and that was that. Six million men are not a few, this wheel. The life of an old man you think about it yourselves if you want to think about it otherwise leave him in peace. Six million, if you please. It's a wheel that turns badly. Let's have no more talk about this wheel, let it turn.

25.

There's a certain resemblance in the nose in the forehead. A woman looks at me, the wife of the butcher of Pavona, and then she says how he resembles him. They're talking about me and him, if you please. Also the mouth the ears the color of the eyes. They are wide open there staring at the Heavens.

All right the nose the forehead the mouth the ears the color of the eyes. If we think about it

ALL MEN RESEMBLE ONE ANOTHER,

the dead especially, but even a living man and a dead one, provided he hasn't been dead too long. Even a man and a woman resemble each other, they have legs arms head, even a dog has legs head a tail, like an elephant. With all due differences a dog closely resembles an elephant, all animals resemble one another and they resemble man. A table doesn't have a head and a tail however it too has legs like us, this is no joking matter.

That is all things resemble one another, the Heavens resemble the sea an apple a melon Italy resembles Japan the Orient the Occident, also the Earth seen from the Moon resembles the Moon seen from the Earth, we know it now with these interplanetary trips and we know other things also. Leave the Earth alone, Rossella says, leave the Moon alone it has nothing to do with it. All right I'll leave the Moon alone, but have you seen the photos of the Earth taken from Cosmos IV? They're beautiful. The Earth seen from far away.

I see it go by at quarter past nine in the evening in the Heavens over Pavona in the midst of the Stars, I greet it and I say you're very lucky to be so high up, Cosmos IV. For you everything is very far away, this dying in the middle of a meadow, this talk of the people, this running of the police, this turning of the Earth under our feet, you feel it turning? This monotony. All you needed was the initial thrust to make you go on for centuries being an artificial satellite for the Russians or for the Americans. Are you Russian or American? From your name you seem American but perhaps you're Russian probably.

How is it there in the stratosphere? I've heard it's very cold but you don't feel the cold. You travel calmly at a hundred seventy degrees below zero centigrade. They say there are

GAMMA RAYS

and other mortal rays, lucky you who don't have any fear of dying. Here a draft is enough to give you a cold. A cold seems nothing, you can die.

[139]

I don't want to hear this resemblance mentioned any more, I put my hands in my pockets and I look away. I feel his eyes looking at me from behind, this priest dressed in black. I'm nervous, if you please. But then what did I come here for? Would you mind telling me what I want? I told you keep away, pretend nothing happened, you're too curious, Giuseppe. All right I'll let them look let them look go ahead, look.

Two eyes are still looking at me, I turn in another direction. This priest dressed in black, Giuseppe, dear friend, how do you expect a priest to be dressed, in black. I don't know him this is the first time I've seen him. It isn't the priest from Pavona he never showed up, he says they'll call me if they want to call me. He says I'm very sorry about what happened in my parish. He says we'll say a prayer if you like for his soul

AVE MARIA GRATIA PLENA.

These exceptional resemblances are the Architect's jokes when the Architect feels like joking. These symmetries. This gossiping. You think you frighten me? I pretend it's nothing, I start whistling, unfortunately I've run out of cigarettes I can't smoke. The Radio is broadcasting Sibelius again on the Third Program, cut it out with this Sibelius. He's bad luck in other words he means trouble.

Wait a minute. They're talking again about my forehead my hands my eyes my face and you let them talk go ahead and talk. Remember one thing you have a head you have a mind, Giuseppe, you can use them as you like. You can carry on the conversation far off at sea, the Tyrrhenian. Do you recall *The Magic Flute?* That's how you must act.

I walk in the meadow again you do nothing but walk. I pick a flower. I pretend to smoke I blow the smoke in people's faces. Leave them alone. All right he's died people die they do nothing but die from morning till night but if man didn't die he would be practically speaking immortal.

This priest dressed in black is looking at me still it would be better if he went off to pray. There are special prayers for the dead Requiem aeternam dona eis Domine, if you please. Now he's chatting with the wife of the butcher, how does he happen to know her? Instead of praying.

WHAT DOES THE BISHOP SAY?

You know you're wasting your time chatting? Go and pray and you'll be better off instead he doesn't move, this priest dressed in black.

The police have unleashed their panther-jeeps in the country around Pavona but I'm here on the scene of the crime, if I'm the one you're hunting for. I must leave without attracting attention, you need a special talent like the Indians of Bengal. You have this special talent however people are staring at me, well let them stare. Watch out for those panthers on the other hand. This countryside it's like walking in the jungle. Luckily panthers don't attack if they aren't attacked, I don't believe it. Perhaps in Asia and in the African Jungle when they are in their natural surroundings, but here they always seem angry, they run at more than eighty miles an hour, they come on you all of a sudden, they're capable of tearing a man limb from limb in two minutes, if you please. They have sharp teeth wide headlights exceptional pickup special tires. They're black. Everybody knows that panthers are ferocious beasts.

Unfortunately here in the Pavona Plain there isn't even a hedge to hide behind which, there are no haystacks manholes masonry walls or dry walls, too bad. There's only me in the whole Plain but my body is no hiding place.

26.

I was walking on foot towards Casale Abbruciato, there was silence all around in the countryside you couldn't even hear a cicada. How tiresome the cicadas are when they start singing. There is always one that begins and then immediately the others all start singing together by the hundreds. It seems a trifling thing, cicadas. Instead they make a deafening noise and there's no means of making them be quiet.

There was silence all around, in the countryside you couldn't hear the cicadas and not even the voice of the Radio which you hear almost always. The silence sometimes you would like to hear at least a voice any old sound, that of your own footsteps as you walk. Why don't I hear my footsteps I can't understand I should hear them. I stop for a moment to listen but I can't hear them if I am still,

TO HEAR MY FOOTSTEPS
I HAVE TO WALK.

Then I walk again on the gravel but I don't hear anything, if you please.

I can't understand what's happening to me, maybe I have rubber soles they don't make any noise. There are certain soft soles, it's like walking barefoot on a rug on tiptoe. But there are no rugs here, a rug in the midst of the countryside on a road covered with gravel, this is no joking matter.

Giuseppe, my dear friend, you haven't rubber soles you know very well they're leather. All right I can have them changed at once by the cobbler in Albano, rubber ones are even better than leather when it rains. But the Sun is out, dear friend. All right the Sun, I said, then I can put on canvas shoes but in some cases there is also rain when the Heavens are serene, in spring and in summer.

I'd almost wish the cicadas would start singing, sometimes the silence is much worse than noise in this case. All right the cicadas but where have the birds gone, I don't hear them chirping. At least an airplane could fly past. With all these airplanes from Pratica di Mare Ciampino and Fiumicino not even one goes by, why don't you go by? What have I done to you? What do you want to do, frighten me by not flying by?

There I see something moving among the branches. It's the leaves, it's the wind that moves them. Then why can't it be heard? I like the sound of the wind in the leaves on the branches. Sometimes it manages to bend even the trunks of the pine trees they are all bent along the seashore. Last year it ripped the roofs off the houses at Torvaianica it picked up the cabins from the bathing establishments and carried them far off.

However that wasn't the normal wind that comes from the sea,

IT WAS A CYCLONE.

It whistled in the Heavens, it rose and it sank, it also picked up a car and threw it into the sea. They never found it again, a Lancia with a lawyer from Palermo inside, the newspaper said.

I'm cold in the Sun, I don't like it. Put up with it. I try running but that doesn't change anything, the silence. I try shouting but why is it I don't hear my voice? If the cicadas don't help me, nobody wants to help me. I can't bear the cicadas they don't want to sing. Keep calm, you have hands you have legs you have arms you're all there you're a man, Giuseppe. But now who am I talking to, whose is this voice behind my back?

I walk towards Casale Abbruciato, I would like to hear some sound even an engine's. At least an engine in the distance. Few automobiles go by few Lambrettas, the road has remained as it was after the American advance when the tanks went by coming from Anzio from the sea. It's full of deep holes. The houses are still in ruins fig trees and thorns have grown inside. The thorns are full of blackberries. A few tanks have been left around they are used as tractors. The Italian Government ought to be told you've downright forgotten this area.

What a longing I have for a chat. There's Rosalma waiting for me leaning out of the window on the second floor, she is signaling to me because she's seen me coming, I make signs too with my hands. Giuseppe, dear friend, see here Rosetta isn't at the window and even if she were how could you see her if you can't see the house? The house is still far away. All right it's far away, from where?

There, now I hear

MUSIC IN THE AIR.

I recognize this voice it's the Radio thank goodness, which is broadcasting *Your Evening Concert* on the Second Program, I mean the silence is broken at last, they're broadcasting Sibelius.

Now I also hear the cicadas singing the birds chirping an airplane in the Heavens, I hear my footsteps on the gravel thanks a lot, to the Radio. All the same, I say, haven't you anything else to broadcast? Sibelius again. These programs are incredibly monotonous. They really could improve them, why don't you improve these musical programs?

27.

I see something moving at the end of the meadow along the Fosso dei Preti, I said, take a look yourself what do you see? Rosaria was there at the window with one eye bandaged, I told you it was a mistake to overdo it, I half blinded you. I can still see lots and lots of flowers, she said, poppies and daisies of every color, clover and alfalfa. No, no, I said, something that's moving at the end of the meadow along the Fosso dei Preti.

My eyesight's a little blurred, she said, but there is something you're right it's moving there at the end, I think I can see

AN AMERICAN TANK.

Cripes, then I wasn't mistaken. And she said I can even see the turret with the Americans' white star and the barrel of the cannon. And you say it in that tone like something normal, a tank with its cannon aimed.

I'll try closing my eyes, you can't see a thing anymore but the air is still trembling. Maybe I think I'm seeing a tank when it's really only a thought, Giuseppe, dear friend, bear in mind that

THOUGHTS DON'T MAKE ANY NOISE,

thoughts don't have engines. Then it's really true, an American tank with its turret and its cannon. Rosa said naturally if there's a tank there's bound to be a cannon. This is exactly what's worrying me and she said you always get lost in details, forget the cannon. How can I forget it? You can't forget it just like that, a cannon. No don't think about it, a tank is something that passes and goes away, look there it's going off. All right it's going off, I said, but I want to know what it is that's going off, a tank or a pure illusion?

Giuseppe, my dear friend, that's an American Sherman with a Diesel engine with a high cubic capacity. Illusions don't go moving around meadows and don't weigh all those tons, can you see the marks of the tracks in the ground? Those are the marks of an American tank.

What year are we in then? Surely we haven't remained back in the war period when the Americans were advancing with the Fifth Army? Maybe we only believe the war is over and instead the countryside is full of soldiers and bombs are about to fall any minute like when the Flying Fortresses went by in the Heavens. The air is vibrating, can't you feel it trembling? I

[148]

can't feel anything, what you can't feel it trembling? Let it tremble the air does what it pleases.

Then how do you explain this thing I see at the end of the meadow, this American tank, tell me because the eye at times can be mistaken. And she said the eye how I love it, why don't we play our game some more? She came over to me with her eye wide. We'll start again tomorrow, I said, we've gone too far already. I understand you don't love me any more. So now she drags in

LOVE.

Wait till this tank goes away and then we'll talk about it and she said keep calm it's going away now. Not all that calm, I said, if it isn't a thought or an illusion what's an American tank doing around here?

I heard, Rosalinda said, that he's a soldier who died during the advance. But if he's dead how can he drive a tank? I didn't make myself clear, it's his soul that can't find peace and comes back to these parts the way the souls of the damned usually do. All right the souls of the damned, I've never heard of a soul dragging along a tank that weighs several tons. Or is it some special kind of soul? I can't tell you about that but I believe souls are all the same. And besides, I said, the tank belongs to the American Army, I mean he's stolen it.

I wouldn't have anything against the idea of a soul that can't find peace coming now and then dressed as an American soldier, but not dragging a whole tank with him. Obviously he can't do without it. And where does he get the gasoline to make it run? It must take plenty of liters I mean gallons as the Americans say and to tell the truth it isn't even a matter of gasoline,

THOSE MONSTERS ARE DRIVEN BY DIESEL OIL.

In other words I don't understand where he gets his oil, this damned soul of this American soldier. You have no idea the amount a tank like that burns it's worse than an airplane. But mind you he can't be nasty, he hasn't shot at anybody and I've never heard of his robbing any filling-station attendant. He ruined a field of potatoes once he must have lost his way.

He died during the advance, she said, right there where you saw him go by at the end of the meadow. Even if he likes coming back every now and then he isn't bothering anybody, except for that peasant that field of potatoes. And does he always drag the tank along with him? You wouldn't expect him to come on foot,

HE COMES FROM VERY FAR AWAY.

But where does he get the oil have you heard anyone say? This is the thing I can't understand where does he get the oil to drive it. It costs a lot. Who gives him the money to pay for it?

Leave him alone, Rosina said, with his tank at the end of the meadow in the midst of the flowers he's going away. And I said one day if he loses his temper he could very well start shooting his cannon, maybe we should go and tell the Italian Army. And she said better not the Italian Army. All right however if he gets mad one day he's likely to cause a massacre. That soldier, I said, that damned soul who comes and goes with his tank, don't think for a moment that a damned soul comes from so far away without knowing what he's come for. I mean he must be sent by somebody, this is no joking matter.

No if you ask me he comes to Italy just to make a trip the way the American tourists come to see the war zones but I've never heard, I said, of them dragging a tank with them. Do as I do, she said, I've already forgotten it. If you forget him it's as if he hadn't been there.

I look out of the window towards the meadow. The Sun has almost set, the wind which before was whistling has calmed down, the chirping blackbird now is silent, the noise has stopped, the noise of the tank. Rosalba says you mustn't even mention it. All right I won't mention it any more, the tank with the damned soul of that American soldier inside it. But you did mention it. I swear I won't say another word about the tank with its turret and its cannon, I've already forgotten it, with the damned soul of that American soldier inside it.

28.

What does he want of me this old man who is following me like a dog and if I turn to the right he turns to the right and if I turn to the left he turns to the left? If I go straight he goes straight, he follows me and doesn't ask himself where I'm going because wherever I go he goes also. What does he want of me? See here I'm a vagabond, see here I walk at random, I turn to the right and I turn to the left without thinking about it and then I'm capable of going back to the place I started from. Why are you following me then? See here I don't have any particular place to go and if you follow me you'll find yourself always back at the beginning, in the end.

The old man continues following me like a shadow, sometimes he makes a little dash and walks in front of me as if he wanted to guess where I'm going but often he makes a mistake because he turns to the right and I turn to the left.

I say, I do what my hands do they're capable of doing terrible things. Watch out for my hands and you'll be better off.

He was mumbling. What is this old man mumbling, what does he want, what do you want? I don't look him in the face I don't want to see him, if he passes in front of me I shut my eyes. I try limping to see what he'll say, nothing. I have one leg shorter than the other, one knee stiff as a corpse, I have trouble walking. I'm lame, if you please.

Now the old man is walking at my side, he trips me up. I don't like it this business of tripping up a lame man. Why are you tripping me? He was coughing, sneezing. He spat on the Earth, he coughed. He scratched himself under his shirt, he kicked at the stones. He tripped me again no, I said, this is something you mustn't do.

We were alone he and I. Automobiles and bicycles could have gone by and they would have raised a lot of dust if there had been any dust, instead they didn't go by and therefore they didn't raise anything. It could have rained and then the dust would have become soaked, the drops would have sunk into the dust and then it would have turned into mud. My shoes and the old man's would have sunk in the mud and we would have ended up each with a foot in a puddle. Then I would have said cripes the mud's got into my shoe. Instead it wasn't raining and it had no intention of raining judging by the clouds that weren't there because the Heavens were serene and silent.

He kept on following me, stubborn. He walked on my shadow, he trampled on it. I'm capable of killing you, I said,

[153]

you're trampling on my shadow, why are you trampling on it? Watch what you're doing, stranger.

I could have turned suddenly and stunned him with my fist and then taken a stone from the culvert by the road and bashed his head in. There weren't any stones in the culvert by the road. Then I could have torn up a stake from the fence. There weren't any stakes and there wasn't even a fence by the edge of the road. We were walking on the grass of a meadow and not on a dusty road. The Radio was broadcasting *Musico-rama*, a medley of songs. They haven't much imagination these directors at the Radio, you haven't much imagination.

What does this old man want of me he wants something surely since he keeps on following me. There he's tripping me again and I'm falling with my hands held out. This is the third time he's played this trick on me, see here I'm losing my patience. Thank goodness patience exists, I said, thank goodness for you I mean for him, the old man. Now however I was really losing my patience. He laughed, he made little noises with his mouth, he mocked me. The air is heavy, there isn't even any Sun it's gone away, it was smart.

I'm in a trap. I hear a sound behind my back, maybe he's picking up a stone in the culvert or a stake from the fence to strike me by stealth. Perhaps he hates me but how can he hate me if he doesn't know me? This is the first time we've seen each other and I haven't even said a word. To hate somebody, you have to make friends first. It's that, friendship, which gives birth to

MORTAL HATRED.

I'm afraid I'm in a cold sweat, and that's nothing to laugh about. But who's laughing who wants to laugh? Nobody around here is laughing. This old man behind my back, I can't find a direction to walk in. I go forward zigzagging in the middle of the meadow, I hasten my steps and I hear his steps behind me, he's hastened his too. Then am I running away? Why of course, Giuseppe, this is called running away what you're doing.

All right I'm running away but I had stopped. There on the road was a black bicycle going by in the darkness of the evening. The old man had stopped too and was looking at me.

A MAN FACING HIS ENEMY.

But to be enemies you have to quarrel. All right let's quarrel then, I said, you need a reason. The old man said we'll find a reason now.

Vietnam for example can be the subject for a quarrel, or else the Middle East question, are you siding with the Arabs or with the Israelis? I'm siding with both, I said. Then the Russians and the Americans who are you siding with the Russians or the Americans? Or with China and its seven hundred million Chinese? What do you have to say about Mao and the Chinese Bomb? Nothing, I said, I say nothing, it's better for us to put everything on the level of the personal insult. All right the personal insult, I said, we don't know each other.

He was holding it hidden in the palm of his hand, a knife, he wanted to kill me with which. I was trying to gain time some-

[155]

how. Then, I said, if we set our thoughts to thinking we produce other thoughts of whatever sort and when we've thought them we can tell each other to our faces and start quarreling. Otherwise we can stay here without talking, we'll just look at each other, we can wait until we've become unbearable to each other. Sometimes it takes only a few minutes, I said, other times it takes years, a whole lifetime, however if a person has patience the moment of hatred arrives. So let's wait then.

Suddenly it's become late, two minutes ago it was early and now it's very late. Then how far have we got? I begin to sense something, a tingling a strange buzz,

IT MUST BE HATRED ARRIVING.

You can feel it, it's like when the train is about to arrive from far away, with your ear on the track. There it's about to arrive. Sometimes the train is late when there's fog or ice when snow falls. During the war it often had to stop inside tunnels for fear of the airplanes. It arrived five even six hours late. When it didn't have time to take shelter and had a direct hit from a bomb, then you had a long wait. Once a train stopped because there was a dog on the tracks.

Go on, why don't you say something? I said. Words lead to quarreling. Why don't you tell me your life story, if you have one. Have you a life story to tell? Or have you nothing? I looked at the knife in his hand. Who are you? I'm Giuseppe, he said. Cripes, this is a thing I don't want to hear any more, this mix-up. That's enough now I'm going away as far as I can, if you please. We'll have to see, the old man said, if I'll let you go.

The police want to know how things ended with that old man. Just a moment, tell me what I must say. You must say everything, Giuseppe. Everything really is a little too much. See here the police want to get to the bottom of things, if there is a bottom. But then, I said, they want to question me, like questioning a suspect.

All right I started to run away. My knee hurt, I couldn't bend it. It's hard to walk with your knee in that condition. It creaked like it was rusted. Rust is no joking matter, in certain circumstances. It's made iron bridges collapse and ships sink, it's brought down High Tension towers and has caused railroad disasters like the one to the train coming from Chiasso.

IT LOST A WHEEL.

The papers published the photographs where you saw a sleeping car standing up-ended in the middle of a wheat field. The passengers were piled one on top of the other like the potatoes in a sack of potatoes. Thirteen people died including the engineer.

Skip the trains, Giuseppe, skip them. What do you mean? Thirteen people died and there were lots of injured, if you please. One lady lost both legs, another lost her head. And you let that worry you? The Bible says

BLESSED IS HE WHO LOSETH HIS HEAD
FOR HE WILL FIND IT AGAIN IN HEAVEN.

[157]

No see here you're mistaken, the Bible says something else about Heaven when it talks about the camel, there's no mention of a head, that lady's.

29.

Giuseppe is dead the Pavona butcher, if you please. They pulled him from the water feet first and they stretched him out on the grass. His eyes were open the lips swollen the face white the hands cold as a serpent's. He drowned in eight inches of water in the Fosso dei Preti near Rossanda's house, Casale Abbruciato.

His wife has shut herself in her house and doesn't want to see anybody, she's right, but the police said very sorry about your grief we have to ask you a few questions. Then she said see here it was an accident, when a man falls into the water and doesn't know how to swim. But what was he doing near the ditch, the butcher? Maybe he fell into the water thinking he was climbing a tree, his wife says. And why did he want to climb a tree if there are no trees around there? That's exactly why he fell into the water, the wife says, leave me alone.

No let's talk about this butcher. He cheated the Public Health Department and the Food Board, he butchered animals that had died of disease, he sold frozen meat for fresh. Don't buy frozen foods, he said, they're bad for you. The big Findus plant near Latina, these Swiss who come to Italy, the butcher said. He wanted to set up a Mammoth Illegal Butchershop to supply the whole area from Albano all the way to the sea.

Maybe it was the Sicilian Mafia that killed him, they're in charge of illegal butchering in all the region of Lazio, they also control the Wholesale Markets. The Mafia, the wife says, what's that, she didn't even know the name of which.

The police want to know if he drank every now and then no sin if he did. Maybe he fell because he had been drinking, he only drank water, the wife says. The police write everything down on sheets of letterhead paper and then send them to Rome to Central Headquarters. But what are they writing? The police act mysterious, they don't say anything to anybody.

These crimes in this area there are already two of them that's too many it's worse than Chicago. Are you hunting for the murderers at least? It seems to me you're wasting your time with the dead man who doesn't need anything anymore, the butcher. Look around, maybe the murderer is only a few steps away from you if you have eyes to see with.

The paper says on the provincial news page the police are on the murderer's trail. Why you're not even sure it's a criminal case. Don't try telling me you're on any trail, I don't believe it. Then, they say, what about those black marks on his neck? The police have found some black marks on the butcher's neck, perhaps they are the marks of the fingers of the murderer's hands.

Nearby there are some footprints on the ground and a pair of eyeglasses they aren't the butcher's whose are they? My husband, the wife says, had very good eyesight, he never wore glasses in his life. He could see far and near.

The Pavona priest has arrived this time he's a parishioner of mine. All right he's a parishioner of yours he worked on Sunday he cursed he never came that is he never went to church. Religion, the wife says, you don't have to go to church.

EVERY NOW AND THEN HE MADE
THE SIGN OF THE CROSS.

Obviously one way or another he had a soul.

The coroner also arrived, looked him over carefully and then said he died by drowning, that is by pulmonary asphyxia. This you could guess without calling the coroner, that he had died by drowning.

The people came from Pavona and from far away, they're the same faces I saw before in the meadow near the Mediaeval Tower, apparently from time to time

THE WORLD REPEATS ITSELF.

The police too are the same ones with the same trucks and the same jeeps. And what am I doing here in the meadow near the Fosso dei Preti? Maybe I'm waiting for somebody. Giuseppe, my dearest friend, what sort of person is this somebody you're waiting for? How can I tell what sort of person he is if he hasn't come yet? At least you know what he wants with you, does he want to do you harm? If that's the case you'd better

[161]

not wait. I don't know anything, I'm not even sure he's a human being.

There's something coming. I hear a strange buzz in the air, that buzzing again. I pretend not to hear it. My ears are deaf in some cases, when they don't want to hear. I turn my eyes and I see the Heavens which are growing dark. They are arriving from all sides. It's them. And what does Giuseppe the fly-killer do in this case? The Necrophila Funeraria is arriving, if you please. What do they pay him for? Why do you pay him, authorities of the City of Albano? Hurry up go and call him.

A black cloud expands and contracts in the Heavens, there are millions and millions of them. Currents are formed eddies little airspouts here and there. The ants run off frightened. The cloud gets blacker all the time. They think they can frighten me, you're mistaken. Come on, I say, if it's me you're after,

EAT ME IF YOU'RE CAPABLE OF IT.

What do you want with me? Look there's a dead man by the Fosso dei Preti, they've just pulled him out of the water, that's where you should go. The butcher.

The cloud fills my eyes and ears with its buzz with its buzzing. I breathe and the flies go down my throat by the hundreds. Then I shouldn't breathe, you think. I've always breathed and I'll breathe as long as I like and you go away if you don't want to be eaten yourselves.

There's a lot of static on the Radio, the red lights of the Santa Palomba tower can't be seen any more. The airplanes going past these parts might have an accident. Luckily they don't go past, they're smart not to go past here.

The cloud covers the Heavens as far as the horizon they're all black. I see some shadows moving on the meadow, they're running away on all sides. I want to know where they're going, where are you going? How black everything is even the Pavona priest. Maybe I'm black too but I don't see myself. Swarms of flies go by like gusts of wind. Somebody opens an umbrella, it's black too.

Sudden currents of cold air arrive you can't tell where it comes from. The first drops of rain sink in the dust and sizzle on the burning Earth. You hear whistles in the air, a crunch, flashes, something is coming down from the Heavens, it's raining. No

IT'S HAILING.

Cripes, it's begun to hail. It isn't flies then, this cloud in the Heavens.

This isn't the first time it's happened. There have been times when hail has fallen bigger than hen's eggs and has ruined everything, it even broke the tiles on the roofs of the houses. It destroyed the Concord grape crop dented automobiles broke street lights killed birds on the wing.

Once the hail killed an ox near Mondoví. Another time an elephant in Düsseldorf, in Germany. Giuseppe, dear friend, what was an elephant doing in Düsseldorf? What do you think he was doing, he wasn't doing anything wrong.

Hail is formed when the vapor in the atmosphere passes through strata of cold air and this happens especially in the spring. Sometimes hail falls together with rain, when these big Roman thunderstorms come. About fifteen miles from here, after Ariccia and Genzano, comes Velletri the rainiest town of the year even the Almanac says so.

Now the Heavens have cleared up, the black cloud is empty now and the air is transparent again. The countryside is all white, so are the roads and the roofs of the houses are completely white. It's beautiful to look at. White is a perfect color but even perfection sometimes leaves much to be desired, all this hail in the Pavona Plain.

This buzz, this buzzing. The Santa Palomba tower has started working again, they're transmitting the EVENING NEWS which says

GREAT HAILSTORM IN THE PAVONA PLAIN,

extensive damage to vines and fruit trees, there are no dead fortunately. What do you mean no dead? That's what you say. Doesn't the butcher count for those people at the Radio? And that other one whose name nobody knows. Giuseppe, dearest friend, first they died and then it hailed. All right first and then, things happen in a chain reaction, the butcher is linked with the Pharaohs, if you please.

People pass along the main street of Pavona, they see the shutter pulled down, there's a sign that says

CLOSED FOR MOURNING.

The wife and son are mourning that is, they're shut up in the house. Tutankhamen is dead. I don't say a thing, I barely knew him.

30.

The Heavens on the other hand were blue. There was a white streak left by an airplane, only that. Flocks of birds went by. Giuseppe, with everything that's happening, you console yourself with very little. What do you mean very little, the Heavens are the biggest thing there is, they can't even be measured because there isn't a number big enough. No recently they've discovered a number bigger than infinity. All right this enormous number but still nobody who knows how to handle it. Every now and then I stop and look at the Heavens. Measure them yourself if you want to measure them.

I'm cold, it's old age, no it's the evening air, it's the years beginning to weigh on me, maybe I have influenza a shudder or two down the spine. No it's the years there are so many. Compared to the blue Heavens they're nothing, they're plenty. All right in some instances old age fills me with great happiness when I tell myself it's the only way to live a long time leave me alone.

Too bad my knees hurt. If I didn't have these knees it would be much better. But I have them and I have to keep them. My back hurts it would be better not to have it. My eyes hurt too with this dazzling light my head hurts. It would be better not to have eyes and head too,

IT WOULD BE BETTER TO HAVE NOTHING.

To go around free and happy as a bird. Giuseppe, dear friend, a bird as you well know has eyes and a head like you. You want to make comparisons and then you get them all wrong, don't make them. Let me get things wrong, birds if I want. They have a head and eyes like you and they grow old too. With this difference, I said, that even when they're old they still fly.

It's rare for anyone to say I saw a very old bird go past, old and young they're all alike in other words they fly in the same way. Maybe if a person pays close attention the difference can be seen when they rise from the Earth. How do very old birds manage to take off? Landing is easier but the take-off requires all the engine's power. That's why there are many more accidents during the take-off than during the landing. Three years ago at Orly one hundred and eleven people lost their lives because of a take-off that went wrong, one of the jet engines exploded. It's fairly unusual but sometimes it happens. On certain minor lines like the Balkan ones or the African the take-off is always dangerous because they still use the old piston-engine planes left over from the war, luckily only a few are left almost all have crashed. Dakotas.

In Spain the Superconstellations are still flying they're very heavy planes and they have a lot of trouble rising from the Earth, sometimes they don't rise one bit and they smash against the barriers. Only a few of them too are left luckily almost all have crashed. Many passengers are dead thanks to them.

Jet airplanes take off much better than the old piston planes but sometimes an engine explodes like at Orly, or else they crash during a take-off for other reasons. Old age is a serious obstacle to flying. However nobody has ever seen a very old bird who couldn't manage to rise from the Earth because of old age.

With human beings, on the other hand, you can tell right away if they are very old even from a distance. They walk along grazing the walls and the hedges dragging their legs after them, their knees hurt them. Some people are ashamed of old age, others are ashamed of death too and when the moment comes they send everybody away and they say

GO AWAY I HAVE TO DIE.

There are certain birds that live for a very long time but in the end old age gets them too. The eagle the falcon the crow and certain South American parrots live more than a hundred years, if you please. After a hundred years they begin to grow old, they lose their feathers. We instead lose our hair through old age. We, in other words human beings.

The cold penetrates the bones, every now and then you feel cold even in full summer when you're going along the street and there's the Sun. Sudden chills come, it's the Eternal Cold advancing. It's like being at the Arctic Circle there's nothing but ice all around, even the houses are of ice and you really don't know where to go. You can't even blow your nose. The Sun can barely be seen and then it disappears, the Heavens are black. In that case it's best to stay well away from this Arctic Circle, let the explorers go there if they want to go.

I'm cold even here while I walk along the road, all my body warmth is being dispersed in the air. Go drink something hot, Giuseppe, go to a bar. I look around for a bar but I can't manage to find one. And yet there are some there were plenty along these roads at night you could see the colored signs. I have to find it before my body becomes completely cold, I can't waste time. I stop a man in the road he doesn't know anything.

Finally I see a sign in the distance that says

CENTRAL BAR.

There I've found a bar, the Central Bar. But central in respect to what? That is what do you think you're in the center of, the World? See here the Center of the World is not around these parts.

Behind the counter there is a barman with a tired face he looks at me as if to say I wonder what this old man wants now, a cup of camomile? Here's the camomile, says the barman. Bonomelli. All right Bonomelli camomile but why are you looking at me like this? I'm tired my hands are trembling my suit is damp my eyes red I'm very pale, but it's still me, I'm Giuseppe known as Giuseppe the same as I've always been.

31.

The police have found this pair of eyeglasses near the Fosso dei Preti lying in the grass on the Earth. If they aren't the butcher's what are these eyeglasses doing there in the grass? They aren't doing anything what do you expect them to be doing? Where do they come from? And the grass and the Earth then where do they come from? Why don't you call the Police Laboratory, let's see what they say, they know as much as we do. The grass and the Earth, sometimes the police make me laugh in this case.

The Police Laboratory has had the lenses measured in a special laboratory which said four diopters on the right and five on the left, he doesn't see very well this character he's shortsighted. They noted it all down in certain very secret files and they sent them to all the police stations from Albano to the sea. The police say now that we've found the eyeglasses

The newspapers say the eyeglasses aren't the butcher's, everybody knows this here in Pavona there's no need for the papers to come and tell us. All right they aren't the butcher's, they aren't mine either if that's what you want to know. I don't wear eyeglasses I wore them a number of years ago but now I see very well, not badly. I used to see very little before I knew Rosangela, now I see even at night like the German pilots during the war. They ate carrots to see in the darkness and the English ate blueberry jam, if you please. I don't need carrots and blueberries nor eyeglasses either you wear them if you want to wear them.

It isn't so easy to find a pair of eyes in the open countryside, they've surely gone to Rome to get lost in the great crowd of the inhabitants. Two million people are no joking matter. You have plenty of hunting to do, two million. There's a train that goes through Pavona on its way to Rome, they can have escaped on it. According to the police they are still in the area, maybe they're hiding behind a pair of smoked lenses. There are also certain eyeglasses with lenses like mirrors which allow you to look but not to be looked at.

The police are stopping everybody who wears eyeglasses and also those who don't wear them but can't see well, they make them get into wagons and they send them off to Rome they don't want to go. The Laboratory works day and night, they don't have any time now to sleep, they measure the eyesight of all these people in their laboratories but they haven't yet found the eyes that correspond to the eyeglasses found on the meadow near the Fosso dei Preti thank goodness.

In Cecchina and in Genzano people threw rocks at the police, they were right.

Then the police put on civilian clothes, they go into the bars, they go dancing on Saturday night, they bowl and go to Mass on Sunday morning. They pretend to travel on the train to Rome, they stroll back and forth in the streets of Pavona with a cigarette in their mouth I mean they pretend to stroll. If a person is a bit absent-minded he doesn't notice anything, he sees these characters smoking or reading the newspapers seated at a table of the Central Bar, they are very calm and don't bother anybody, but if you look carefully

IT'S LIKE BEING IN CHICAGO IN THE DAYS OF AL CAPONE

when people shot at one another in the streets. You had to stay behind locked doors in your house for whole weeks. The gangsters were lying in wait at the corner of the street or they drove up in a car shooting volleys from the windows. You can't even go to the bar or the restaurant or have yourself shaved by the barber. While you're sitting peacefully in the chair with your face lathered, a character comes in with a machine gun in his hand and shoots you point blank. He can easily mistake me for somebody else this character with the machine gun in his hand if my face is lathered. Those people don't think twice before they shoot. A city like this is a place that doesn't appeal to me, I'm going away. What am I doing here in Chicago? I'm going back to Italy, if you please.

But do you at least know what they're like these eyes that correspond to the lenses of the eyeglasses that you found in the meadow near the Fosso dei Preti where the butcher died?

Diopters all right but there are all sorts of eyes, they can have a thousand different shades. They run from yellow to green to orange, they can have all the colors of the rainbow, they can be blue as the sea and green as the Heavens, grey brown violet and other colors. Also black. In certain cases the right eye is one color and the left a completely different one and vice versa in infinite combinations.

You'd have to know if these eyes you're hunting for see worse from a distance or from nearby, there are a number of ways of seeing badly. Many people wear eyeglasses and don't need them, others wear eyeglasses with the wrong lenses.

Some men have a glass eye, others have both eyes of glass and nobody notices it. They're made very well they seem real, the only difference is that they can't see. Now they've even invented synchronized glass eyes. These characters who have glass eyes almost always wear eyeglasses and the lenses can be any way they please.

That is it's not easy to find a murderer through a pair of eyeglasses. Go around, have people throw rocks at you, maybe the eyes you're hunting for are there reading the newspaper and they are raised every now and then to look at you, they're laughing in your face and you don't even realize it.

32.

I'm not coming to Rome you go if you want to go there. They want to take me to Rome to talk with the men in the Police Laboratory I don't know the intentions of whom. They're odd characters why don't they come here to Pavona if they want to talk to me? It takes a quarter of an hour or otherwise they can telephone me. If they don't telephone me so much the better just so they leave me alone.

I know what Police Laboratory men are like, and they don't appeal to me. When they get their hands on somebody they don't let him go again, they stick to him like a leech also known vulgarly as

THE BLOODSUCKER

a repulsive animal that sucks people's blood. It resembles the snail without having a shell like a snail, it has a mouth like a suction cup three strong jaws eighty little teeth very sharp to pierce the skin. Once it's attached it doesn't stop sucking. It swells until it bursts and the human being can die from bleeding to death.

Once upon a time leeches were used in hospitals instead of surgical blood-letting for diseases like pneumonia cerebral hemorrhage and other types of hemorrhage and diseases like phlebitis and acute nephritis. There were leech farms in all the cities but many had leeches sent from Paris. Today you can easily find them at liberty in the streets of the Capital towards evening, in Via Capo le Case in Via del Tritone in Via Veneto and near the Railroad Station. Or else farther away at Tor di Quinto near the Ponte Milvio. There you find them by the hundreds.

Also on the Great Ring Road in the stretch that connects the Superhighway to the Superhighway for Naples and for Milan. They're sitting on the curbstones with cigarettes in their mouths, they wear gaudy dresses so they can be seen at a distance, they keep their legs crossed to attract attention. For truck drivers they make special prices.

The ones on the Via Veneto are the best and also the most expensive, they can cost up to fifty thousand lire for an evening. Naturally the rates change according to the season, during the summer they increase a lot because of the American tourists. The police every now and then make a raid.

I'm not going to Rome you go if you want to. I understand perfectly well you want to incriminate me. You don't have the evidence, all you have is a pair of eyeglasses. You have to prove they're mine and I'll prove to you they're not. I can find a pair of eyeglasses myself if I start hunting. If I don't find them I can go and buy them with all the diopters I want.

Giuseppe, dear friend, you can't treat the police this way, in your opinion how should I treat them? You're trembling while you talk, the police make you tremble. All right I'm trembling, with this voice behind me I'm tired. See here maybe I can't bear any more. A man starts trembling in certain situations when he's cold, for example. Giuseppe, we're in full summer and it's hot, even the tar on the streets has melted. At Circeo a pine wood burned up from spontaneous combustion.

All right the Circeo pine wood and spontaneous combustion, anyway I'm not going to Rome you go. But if you want some advice give the Capital a wide berth if you value your life. Otherwise

YOU'LL BE BLOWN SKY HIGH ONE AND ALL,

you and your trucks and your jeeps. I warn you I mean I've already warned you, Rome in a little while is going to blow up, it's on the verge of blowing up.

In Via Nazionale the terrain has given way and some cracks have opened, that's what the newspapers say. No, it happened in a different way, that is the terrain didn't give way it swelled up. This can be seen by certain fissures in the tar towards the top and not towards the bottom.

About halfway down Via dei Serpenti if you look closely the cracks between the slabs of the sidewalk have widened. This means the Earth is growing and is swelling, if you please. Something is moving underground underrome. Also in other points of the city you can notice little indications of the same phenomenon, very fine cracks almost imperceptible swellings. Those who go by every day aren't even aware of it but meanwhile

THE EARTH IS MOVING.

At such times it's a good idea to pay attention to the animals, they have a special sensitivity. The rats for example what do they say I mean what are they doing? If they abandon a ship that's about to sink they also abandon a city that's about to blow up. Human beings are absent-minded they don't notice what's happening under their very feet.

An engineer from the Socony Vacuum of Latina one day was talking about these things in other words he was talking about Rome. He said the cities sometimes build up very high degrees of tension. It isn't a question of electricity but of currents that come from the Center of the Earth we don't know the nature of which. This is what he said the engineer from Latina.

Maybe I should act as if nothing has happened and say go on to Rome don't worry, nothing's going to happen anyway. Instead I tell you again watch out because Rome can blow up any minute. The people from City Hall have issued bulletins to calm the populace are very upset, they're right. They can say what they like in their bulletins, the danger is still very serious. They say for thousands of years Rome has remained standing and it's never blown up, there's the Colosseum the Arch of Titus and the Baths of Caracalla. There's also the Vatican with the Pope but that'll blow sky high too along with the Colosseum the Arch of Titus and the Baths of Caracalla. Not even Monte Mario will remain standing.

The last time I crossed Piazza Colonna, it was half past three in the afternoon, you could hear a strange buzz in the air like when you're walking by a factory, an electric mill. They're things you don't hear with your ears, you perceive them God knows how like horses do earthquakes. Dogs also hear earthquakes a few hours in advance. I heard this strange buzz this buzzing that came from the depths of the Earth but it's obvious it's not a question of an earthquake now,

IT'S A QUESTION OF SOMETHING ELSE.

33.

You go along the paved road that crosses the Valley of Ariccia in a northeasterly direction and you arrive at the so-called Osteriaccia of Ariccia three hundred eighteen meters above sea level according to the Topographical Map of the Military Topographical Institute. Here we find ourselves facing an ancient arch. Probably it was the entrance to a villa but now the villa no longer exists there's a field of turnips. You pass along the flank of the arch and you find yourself on a side road, you can turn left or right according to where you want to go towards Albano or towards Genzano.

We turn to the right, uphill on a very narrow road, with a wall running along the side of which. On this wall there's a white marble sign that says

APPIAN WAY.

Everyone went by here before Pius IX had the famous Ariccia bridge built which has fallen down.

We proceed slowly along the Appian Way is very narrow and full of uphill curves. After half a mile the Map says Le Bandelle and a bit farther on it says Podere Campana. You proceed for another half mile, the road keeps to the slope of the hill. The Map doesn't say anything else. We are about halfway between Ariccia and Genzano and here I am very worried. You can blow up everything in a minute, a mere nothing would suffice at this point. A nothing in other words a match.

A flame would rise from the Earth, a frightful explosion an earthquake. The houses of Ariccia and of Genzano would be severely damaged and even in Rome the Romans would feel the Earth tremble beneath their feet. In fact there beside the road a few yards farther down

THERE'S A POWDER MAGAZINE.

I'm holding in my lips a burnt-out cigarette. You don't want to light it I hope, says Rosella, standing at a safe distance. I take out a box of matches. I could light one. I open the box, in the silence you can hear the box slide open. I take a match between my fingers, I rest it lightly against the sandpaper.

WATCH OUT.

I hold my breath. I see, Rossana says, you want to frighten me. Let's see what I'm capable of doing. All right, here I could write the words The End or rather somebody else would have to write them, after the explosion. Instead I put the match back in the box, I put the box back in my pants pocket. My cigarette is still unlit and the Heavens serene, two swallows pass and I watch them pass. It was a close shave, if you please.

I ran quite a risk but now the danger's past. It would have been a premature end, Rossana says, premature with respect to what? Respect to whom? Who is this character with respect to whom it would have been a premature end? Do I know this individual? I'd like to know the name of whom. I don't know who you're talking about, she says from a distance.

You can proceed along the Appian Way towards Genzano. On the right there are clumps of acacia that block the view otherwise you would see the whole Plain all the way to the sea. You could also see the houses of Pavona and the railroad embankment, the vineyards green or red according to the season and the plantations of olive trees. Instead you can't see anything because of these clumps of acacia that flank the road.

Roselda says you read the Map wrong here it says Abandoned Powder Magazine. Let's admit it's been abandoned as the Topographical Map of the Military Topographical Institute says, still I don't trust these military topographers they may have made a mistake. There could be a bit of dynamite left or some gunpowder.

We go on another hundred yards or so there's a pile of refuse, little boxes of plastic and of tin rags cardboard cartons rusty wire broken bottles, the people of Genzano come here to throw things away at night when nobody sees them. Here along the Appian Way they've made a Great Garbage Heap, you can smell the stink from far away.

A few yards beyond the garbage heap there's a cement pole and a sign with a skull and two crossed bones. It reads

DANGER.

Obviously the High Tension wires pass by here. All you have to do is touch them with one finger. Here again everything could end the story along with its protagonist perhaps.

I go over over and touch the pole, I could climb up and then stretch out my hand. I'd need a ladder. If I don't find a ladder I can't die unless I manage to scramble up with my hands and legs the way the peasants do. But why should I make all this effort?

I don't even know if I'd like to die all charred. I'm still here hesitating looking at this skull with the crossed bones, there's nothing to joke about with a sign like this. A fast car goes by and a pickup truck loaded with turnips, maybe it's going to the market at Genzano. My legs begin to walk, I move away from the pole, another narrow escape.

WHO SHOULD I THANK?

34.

Giuseppe has died too the fly-killer of the City of Albano, if you please. A peasant from Cecchina was going by under the Ariccia bridge at exactly six o'clock in the morning with a load of turnips he was taking to the market at Genzano. The Appian Way passes under the Ariccia bridge. The Heavens were serene but that doesn't mean anything, they could have been stormy and it wouldn't have changed things.

I heard a whistle in the air, says the peasant from Cecchina, like during the war when the American bombs were falling I remember it well that way of whistling I still have it in my ears after all this time has gone by. I looked up and I saw him plunging down from the bridge on his black bicycle, he seemed to be flying in the air the way birds fly when they start flying.

The Ariccia bridge had fallen down during the night of

January 17 without a word to anybody but with a lot of noise. During the war the Germans had blown it up with mines and then it had been badly rebuilt with stones and concrete, they should have built it with reinforced concrete a bridge like that two hundred feet high, if you please. Pius IX had built it in his time on the model of the Roman ones with three orders of arches. The famous arches that can be seen from the distance, from the Plain. Now they aren't seen any more because they've collapsed.

Then, says the peasant from Cecchina, I stopped and went to see the stones were stained red the head bashed in the wheels crumpled the body shattered the frame twisted the arms and legs unscrewed the neck almost torn from the rest of the body the handlebars had flown far away. I went back to the road and I started vomiting, this is what the peasant from Cecchina says who was going by under the Ariccia bridge at six o'clock in the morning with his load of turnips he was taking to the market at Genzano.

Giuseppe knew very well that the Ariccia bridge was broken and that means he didn't fall by accident he threw himself off. There are also arrows saying turn right on the Cecchina road and then go up to Genzano again you are obliged to make this detour. There in front of the bridge there are sawhorses with signs

BRIDGE OUT.

You can see them from the distance, they're painted red.

Then don't come telling me that this time it was a crime, Giuseppe the fly-killer threw himself off the bridge. Or else it was an accident that is he didn't see the signs he couldn't see very well without his glasses.

His son says that he killed himself on purpose out of spite in other words in protest against the City of Albano they wouldn't buy him a motor-driven pump, I don't believe it. A man can kill himself for whatever reason he pleases but for a motor-driven pump, this is no joking matter. The son says he bore a grudge. But the City of Albano it isn't their fault if they've gone into debt up to their necks and don't know how to manage, poor things, they have to economize even in little matters, a motor-driven pump.

About ten days before throwing himself off the bridge Giuseppe was poisoned it had never happened in the whole time he had been a fly-killer. He had started pumping the poisoned molasses against the wind, they found him on the ground half dead behind a myrtle hedge. His eyes were wide foam around his mouth and his tongue swollen like a balloon.

He was delirious in the ambulance that took him to the hospital. He said this buzz in my ears take it away I don't want to see it. Who colored the air boiling red? Where and when are you taking me? This light in my eyes why don't you make it keep quiet? What is this smell? Paint it some other color. No this isn't the buzzing of flies, he said, it's

THE NOISE OF THE EXPANDING UNIVERSE

the way Hindus hear it. He had been in India during the war as a prisoner.

Explain to me carefully what this noise is like, said the Pavona priest, he was maddeningly curious. I can believe it, the noise of the expanding Universe. It's like the clouds when they race in the Heavens, said Giuseppe, I can't understand, the Pavona priest said, or else like the rustling of lots of very fine chains that are motionless in a meadow. Like the electricity wires when the wind isn't blowing or the Sun's rays going through a poplar woods in summer.

I hear the mysterious syllable of creation, he could hear it in the air. He raved in his room at the Albano Hospital and said I'm sure the Center of the World is around these parts here in this neighborhood, maybe in the Pavona Plain. The priest was profoundly disturbed and said this syllable you say you hear in the air why don't you write it down on a slip of paper?

Giuseppe with pencil in hand and his hand trembling had written

OM

now I know as much as I did before, the Pavona priest had said. Om Hling Svaa, said Giuseppe. Handarp Fao and other strange things. FAO is the Food and Agriculture Organization of the United Nations, said the Pavona priest he was offended.

He said watch out you're crushing me to the people at the Albano Hospital, keep your fingers to yourself don't tear my wings off. Bring me a little jam or some decomposing matter. Also a bit of molasses provided it isn't poisoned.

He seemed completely cured when they sent him home that is his mind was working as it had always worked badly. One morning he got on his black bicycle and started pedaling towards the Ariccia bridge. There below by chance a peasant from Cecchina was going by with a load of turnips he was taking to the market at Genzano. It was exactly six o'clock in the morning.

The police say luckily this time it isn't a crime. All right it isn't a crime however all of these Giuseppes come to a bad end, if you please. First the butcher drowned and now this other one the fly-killer, smashed to bits. Giuseppe is a name I don't like, cripes I'm worried.

35.

I went to the sea and I stayed for hours and hours on the beach
to listen to the sound of the waves at Torvaianica but along
with the waves came his voice behind my back. Giuseppe
haven't you noticed anything, he said. What? and then I ran
off I didn't want to hear it. The voice persecuted me, you're
dissolving like a licorice stick, it said. I jumped from one place
to another, from the beach to the pine woods and then to the
Plain, I didn't want to hear it that voice behind my back.

You're aging visibly, it said, your skin's peeling off, your
teeth and hair are falling out, your bones creak in every joint.
All right I have a touch of arthritis I've always had it that isn't
all, the voice said. It seems to give you pleasure, I said, but still
you can't break free of me.

Giuseppe, dear friend, if you go on like this you'll be a corpse in a matter of days. All right you could keep quiet and instead he went on. Nobody notices it when it happens to him, he said, you only see it when it happens to other people and not to you that is you become dispersed in the air and you believe you're still present you'd do better to keep quiet. And instead you're absent. It's really true, I said, cripes death is nothing to joke with it's no joking matter and then I made another try to escape.

Every now and then Rosalia's voice broke in from the distance, you want to interfere too? I told you about the Earth when it isn't cultivated I've dried up like that. I cultivated you in my way as best I could, in any case all right so much the worse I'll make do with Springtime Milk from the Frosinone Milk Products Co. You surely don't mean to compare me to the Frosinone Milk Products Co., she said, don't worry I'm not comparing anybody, comparisons.

Let's hope it doesn't rain, I said, this mackerel-sky. I had made a jump all the way to Albano where there was a program of

GREAT CELEBRATIONS

for the feast of the Blessed Virgin of the Rotonda in the Centenary of the Liberation of the town of Albano from the Cholera.

After a hundred years the inhabitants of Albano have remembered the cholera and they're holding this big celebration with a Diocesan Procession and Holy Mass celebrated by the Cardinal Vicar who will come especially from Rome, why haven't you invited the Pope too? You could have invited him and maybe he would have come, the people in Pavona did last year. They didn't believe it and the Pope arrived in person.

The streets of Albano are full of signs that say this afternoon Great Motorcycle Gymkhana and Cross Country Steeplechase and immediately afterwards Outdoor Rosary in the middle of the meadow I like all this confusion in the streets of Albano, I mingle with the noise. The people are very excited, Albano saved from Cholera, this is no joking matter.

The Holy Image of the Madonna will pass through the streets of the city, in Piazza Mazzini tickets will be placed on sale for the Lottery you might win a Fiat or a leather Armchair put up by the Fajella Furniture Company of Latina. In the evening Tug of War Lucky Dip and then Great Fireworks Display compliments of the Stacchini company, watch out that company manufactures explosives they can destroy Albano in a moment. Stacchini are the bomb people, if you please, the famous Stacchini bombs.

Afterwards comes an Artistic Variety Show with the participation of Wellknown Artists of Radio and Television, but who are these Wellknown Artists? Do you want to surprise us or is this a trick to attract people? And what is Artistic Variety? Explain yourselves better and you'll be better off.

The big sign says and in conclusion Dramatic Performance of Roman Dialect Theatre and Solemn Requiem High Mass. But why this mixing of Sacred and Profane? And for who might the Requiem Mass be? For those dead of cholera a hundred years ago or for somebody else? For who? Tell things

[189]

properly, first and last name. First name at least. And don't alarm people for nothing.

The voice has followed me even here in the midst of the great confusion of the feast day, I have come back down into the Plain, I am walking along the Fosso dei Preti. You can walk along the road calmly, this voice says again behind my back, nobody sees you anyway. All right nobody sees me because they don't want to see me.

The voice was persecuting me, I stopped up my ears, be quiet I don't want to hear you. If things were as you say you wouldn't go around so easily up and down the Plain and the voice said you arrive at the sea from Albano and vice versa in less than a minute as if you were traveling by plane does it seem natural to you? You're forgetting, I said, my bicycle, I could have installed a motor. The voice laughed from the distance, the bicycle's tires are baked by the sun, it's all rusty it's nothing but an abandoned wreck.

You've got yourself in a bad spot, Giuseppe, the voice said again behind my back, let's not exaggerate now I'm going to talk to Rosmunda. I look around and I can't see the house, Casale Abbruciato. Either the house doesn't exist any more or I don't exist any more, at this point. Or has the house become transparent? This is where you're wrong, the transparent one is you, the voice says again behind my back, you must have noticed that nobody speaks to you. You move among people and it's as if nobody were going by. That may be true, I said, I don't care at all about being looked at, I go calmly on my way, not all that calmly.

I look around and nothing is changed, the Sun is in its place and isn't moving, the Earth has remained exactly the same, the roads go where they have always gone,

THE WIND BLOWS WHERE IT PLEASES.

But where is the wind when it isn't blowing? The Encyclopaedias don't say. The Radio never talks about it why don't you talk about the wind sometimes instead of Sibelius? People know everything about everything or almost, but they don't know that certain winds are faster than a racing car, a Ferrari. For example the Bora that blows in Trieste where there aren't even any Superhighways.

Also the famous Monsoons in the Indian Ocean are very fast but they are far away, nobody ever heard of a Monsoon at Pavona otherwise who knows where I would have flown on high in the Heavens like an airplane I enjoy flying. If I look down I see the whole panorama with the red roofs of the houses the roads the canals the plowed fields the cities the little villages lost in the mountains, maybe from here you can also see the Italian Grid, unfortunately I can't see it

I'VE LOST MY EYEGLASSES.

Giuseppe you're spinning your wheels, you seem to me like a flag that flaps in the wind, says the voice behind my back. There's nothing wrong with that, I said, a flag. You'd do better to settle on a piece of Earth and finally lay your bones to rest, if you have them. Now the police have gone away with their wagons and their panther-jeeps, with their tails between their legs, I don't believe it. They've left tire marks on the damp Earth in the direction of Rome. See here it hasn't rained around these parts for several days, I said, the Earth isn't damp. It will become damp when it rains. All right then these tire marks can easily be eliminated with a spade or even bare hands. And if you eliminate them, the voice behind my back said, the police haven't gone away, they are still underfoot. You're better off letting them go I mean having let them go.

I don't understand, I said, why I'm better off what do you want I have nothing to fear at this point. Giuseppe, dear friend, you'll see something more will happen, once it begins it's a chain. All right a chain, I said, I have nothing to do with it I want nothing to do with which.

36.

Now cripes you're exaggerating.

THE BEACH ATTENDANT TOO.

Another Giuseppe gone, one after the other.

He had seen something floating on the water of the sea, a big black stain left there by some passing tanker. Every now and then in the Tyrrhenian tankers go by and clean their tanks on the high seas. If the oil comes to the beach it gets mixed with the sand, it's worse than shit. People don't come to swim any more like on the French Coast when the famous tanker the Torrey Canyon sank the sand became all black.

A beach attendant on his beach, he picks up the greasy paper the empty beer and Coca-Cola bottles, there are people who bring a flask of wine with them and when it's empty they smash it on the beach, why did you smash it? The bits of glass become mixed with the sand and in the evening all the bathers find their feet cut, they look at their soles and they say funny these cuts. Not all that funny, bits of broken flask mixed with the sand.

There are signs that say forbidden to leave sharp objects on the sand, also waste paper and leftover food are forbidden, nobody pays any attention. People on the Italian beaches are often very badly behaved.

Giuseppe had got on to the float, I want to see this oil what it's doing, if it's planning to dirty up my beach which is dirty enough already. Oil can ruin a beach for the whole season like it happened on the French Coast when that famous tanker sank in the Atlantic.

It was eight-thirty in the evening on the beach of the Seaview Baths of the Lido di Lavinio. His grandfather the attendant's was there watching, he had lighted a cigar stub every now and then it went out he lighted it again. Giuseppe rowed the old man smoked the Sun slowly set.

On the terrace of the Seaview Baths seven or eight people were seated at the tables, they were looking towards the sea. The water was calm and the Heavens serene the Sun continued setting. But are you sure you haven't got mixed up the Sun is red too when it sets. They all answer in chorus we're sure, we saw

A BALL OF FIRE.

It was floating on the water and the water was steaming from the heat. You could see the red glints on the sea. See here it must have been the glints of the Sun they're red too, we can't be mistaken.

A carabiniere colonel was the first to see it, he said to his wife turn around and look a ball of fire on the sea. The wife turned around and said yes it really is a ball of fire. There were also two French girls and they also said in French there's a ball of fire floating on the sea.

You say the beach attendant wanted to burn the oil to keep it from coming on to the beach so he burned himself up too, all right that is the official version. That is he came close in the boat to the oil and lighted it with a match, I don't believe it. It must have been somebody else who set fire to it going by in a motorboat. In other words

IT WAS YOU.

Then you ran off pretending you were just arriving. Now you go around saying we hurried and we did everything possible to save him but what sort of everything did you do? You threw a match in the oil and then you let him burn, the beach attendant, if you please. You're lucky that on water you can't leave fingerprints.

The divers arrived too and started hunting under the water what do you think you're going to find? Fish and salt water. If you go and touch the bottom you can also dredge up some Roman amphoras. You'll never find the corpse, it was burned up. It only takes a few minutes to burn a human body they burn very easily, the people in the crematory ovens knew that and you know it too how long it takes to burn a human body.

I bet it was you in the other cases too. This isn't the first time you've struck in this area, your conscience is stained with blood. I'll tell you what you all are

MURDERERS IN THE TRUE SENSE OF THE WORD.

This chain of crimes, these sudden deaths, you are well organized. They tell me you pay people to keep them quiet.

The grandfather is keeping quiet, he sits there on the beach and stares into the distance. I try asking him some questions and he looks at me terrified. What have you done to him? Have you threatened him? He turns toward the sea and tries to light his cigar stub it is very damp. He has used up a whole box of matches and he'll use up another before dying. These Italian cigars you should ask the State Tobacco Monopoly why do you make them so badly? If they're not damp they're moldy. Sometimes they have holes, they look worm-eaten. On the box you write Light and instead they're Dark. Despite the reputation they have,

THEY CAN'T BE SMOKED.

Don't complain then if people prefer French cigarettes with black tobacco they're much better than your cigars. Or else the black Brazilian cigars.

I see the old man's eyes lost in distant thoughts, sometimes old people become lost in their thoughts. It's a way of traveling better than the train or the airplane. But what are these thoughts like? Why is he keeping quiet?

And then you organized this fake funeral and you also sent a wreath of chrysanthemums but why didn't you write your name on the gold ribbon? This is how Al Capone did, first you kill them and then you send flowers.

YOU'RE WORSE THAN AMERICAN GANGSTERS.

And besides, if you're so smart, catch me if you can. You'll never find me, with all your organization. I run like the wind, now I'm here and a minute later at Albano. I pass even where there aren't any roads. I run through the countryside back and forth with no effort, free and solitary as a rhinoceros. With the difference that he weighs a ton or so and I'm light as air.

37.

I see a little procession beyond the hedge, a black automobile a dog a woman three men on foot a priest. There is also a boy on a bicycle pedaling on tiptoe. Where are they going where are you going where you please go ahead.

But why don't you say something why don't you chat? You must know one another if you go around all together or have you nothing to say? That happens. However I'd like to see you speak, or have you lost the power of speech? Stop keeping quiet, you're like embalmed mummies.

In the Heavens a flight of black birds passes if you look into the air you'll see them or don't you want to see them? The Ancient Romans looked at them before setting out on a journey. You can look at them too if they looked at them. If you don't want to look at them do as you please they'll go on flying all the same.

I don't want to know where you're going to some specific place or just at random? Go where you please if you continue in this direction you'll reach the sea, do you know how to swim? Do you plan to turn at a certain point or do you mean to continue in a straight line for your whole lives? If you do you'll end up

CIRCLING THE PLANET.

Then you'd better stop because you're already where you'll arrive in the end. Mind you there are a lot of obstacles to overcome, the sea the mountains. Are you following Meridian Lines or Parallels? Be careful the Meridians all pass by the Pole and I advise you to keep away from it.

If instead you turn somewhere what happened to that file of ants could also happen to you. That is the ant in the lead made a mistake and started following the last ant in line. They kept going around in a circle, they thought they would arrive somewhere and they never arrived there. In the end they died one by one of fatigue and hunger, if you please. Watch out that it doesn't happen to you too the way it did with that file of ants.

You have such a strange look, you're clumsy in your walking, you go on foot and you seem to be pedaling, why are you acting like this? I don't want to know. You keep your eyes down I mean you look down at the Earth, why? Are you embarrassed? What sad faces you have, has something happened? By any chance

HAS SOMEBODY DIED AROUND THESE PARTS?

[199]

Who was he what was his name what did he do for a living how old was he where are you carrying him? I don't want to know. Do I know him by any chance? Tell me frankly, is what you're doing a funeral? But in that case why is the priest at the end instead of in the lead with the Crucifix in his hand? And why aren't you crying? There are rules to be observed and it seems to me you're not observing them. Do what you like.

Has there been an accident perhaps? There are so many, you have to be very careful. You can be electrocuted by electrical current, run over by a passing automobile, you can fall in a ditch and die by drowning, also there are many vipers in the countryside. Sometimes a pin is enough to make a man die or a little piece of lead.

HUMAN FRAGILITY.

Or are you simply taking a walk and the priest is with you by pure chance? But then why is that woman dressed in black? I don't want to know however people don't go around dressed in black in daylight. Black at night or in the evening.

A little while ago there it was daylight and now it still isn't dark however this car has its headlights on. They've also turned on the lights along the road but what time is it then? I don't want to know. When I know the time and I don't know what's happening at that time. They must have watches the people at the Pavona Town Hall if they've turned on the lights before the Sun has set there must be a reason.

There are many holes in the road a bit of dirt and gravel wouldn't do any harm. When it rains they fill with water and become puddles, the dust becomes mud and walking is hard. Change roads if you don't like this one.

The procession goes along slowly, obviously it's in no hurry to arrive. Where are you going and why? Don't tell me I don't want to know. Maybe it's a secret and then you're right to keep quiet, up to a point. If you take me with you I'll follow you without saying a word without asking indiscreet questions.

You've trampled a beetle underfoot. He's still there on the Earth crushed, some white stuff has come out of his belly. Four other beetles came up, they stopped to look and then they ate this white suff that came out of the belly of the beetle you crushed. I'm not saying anything. They are strange animals, they have wings and they can't fly, otherwise he would have flown away and you wouldn't have crushed him. Instead you've also crushed the four beetles who came to eat the white stuff from the belly of the first beetle, if you please.

My knees hurt from walking. We've come a long way and we still haven't arrived anywhere. Maybe because we're going slowly, for hours and hours we've been walking. Couldn't we hasten our steps and perhaps finally arrive? But where if you won't tell me where we're going. Or by chance are we walking in a circle? We won't end up like that file of ants, I hope.

If I come with you I must know where I'm going. Where are you taking me? Giuseppe, dear friend, to a quiet place. All right but what's it called, it must have a name or is it one of those places that aren't marked even on the Maps of the Military Topographical Institute? Is it very far away? It's nearer the Earth than the sea, it's very cool, there's shade in every season. You sound like the Sybil to me, I said, this voice behind my back I don't like the things you say I mean I don't like you very much at all.

When it comes to speaking, you don't want to speak. You're right. Still you have a worried look. What's happening to you? Something serious and unexpected or the normal concerns of life? What life, Giuseppe, you have your nerve calling it that. All right I'll call it something else, what shall I call it? Maybe you'd be better off not calling it anything in this instance.

All right you don't want to talk you're smart to keep quiet while you go on walking. Now the voice of the Radio begins again *This Evening's Programs*. Sibelius again Sibelius this

VALSE TRISTE

always that. Ladies like it, what do you find in it? Does it recall your childhood or what, your first love? Sometimes childhood is involved in these preferences often. However there aren't only ladies in this World, I say this for the benefit of the people at the Radio.

38.

Giuseppe, dear friend, no dear friend we're not friends any more at this point. Why, once upon a time we were inseparable like two brothers and now all of a sudden. All right like two brothers things have changed, I said, characters like you you know what you are? I'm not telling you so as not to quarrel let's go ahead and quarrel all right

YOU'RE A PARASITE.

Then bear in mind, Giuseppe, there are parasites in this World and then there are also the parasites' parasites, there are fleas that have lice.

All right lice, I said, at least they don't act as informers they don't side with the police. Giuseppe, there are certain people who believe they see the police everywhere. To begin with, I said, I don't like to be called certain people. Then how do you explain the fact that the police always know where I go and I always find them on top of me by surprise? The voice laughed, there's not all that much to laugh about. See here I've lost my temper, I said, see here I'll bash your face in, if you have one. That depends on whether I'll allow it to be bashed in. See here I'll drive you away, I said, what are we together for anyway? At a certain point each goes his own way, now I'm going mine, go ahead.

Every now and then the voice moves away, I don't hear it any more behind my back. I sit down on a stone under a tree behind a hedge near a ditch along the road that leads to the Pavona Station. I'll take you to the Station if you want to catch the train, I said. I walk on the paved road, I listen to the wind that whistles in my ears. You'll be sorry, he said, alone in the night when it rains and the wind whistles in your ears. It was raining. Now he sneezed, you've caught a cold, I said, think about your health, you think about your own.

Now I could hear that the voice was trembling. Don't we want to think it over, he said, perhaps we were joking. At times people amuse themselves by joking. Not at all, I said, you're going away I don't want to see you any more I mean I don't want to hear you any more. Why don't we stay here and talk it over, he said, sitting on a stone under a tree sheltered if it rains, look here sometimes decisions are made in haste. Nobody ever heard, he said, of one person being divided in two, it would be the first time it's happened.

There are certain worms, I said, that are divided even in four, they have their life organized in a circular way so if you cut them into so many pieces each piece lives on its own and little by little becomes an independent worm. If somebody comes up with a knife he laughs and says go ahead and cut

INSTEAD OF ONE I'LL BECOME TWO.

There are also worms, I said, that divide spontaneously like the so-called Tapeworm. There, I said, we can also divide spontaneously like him.

Let's wait a moment, said the voice behind my back, and I said that's enough now we're going to the Station and he complained you make me leave so suddenly, I take back what I said if I offended you. Nothing doing no going back, I like the World for this very reason because there are those who go and those who come, because there's movement in all directions. I don't understand, he said, what you're hoping to do I hope what I please.

He had started crying, cripes you're crying now? He was crying. I'm not crying, he said, in fact when I think about it I'm very pleased then so much the better. I'm worried about you, he said, leaving you alone, I'm sorry. Look here, I said, if you don't leave I'm leaving. I'll start traveling and I'll go around the World luckily it's very big, there's plenty of traveling to do.

Now he was sobbing, we were close to the Pavona Station, you could hear the little bell along the track announcing the arrival of the train. You're sending me to Rome, he said, I don't like it. If you want, you can also go from Rome to Milan.

I walk slowly along the road the bar at the crossing is already lowered, I stoop under the bar and cross the tracks.

[205]

The train arrives with its noise of a train on the tracks, there are travelers looking out the windows, they are going to Rome, there are lots of people who like traveling. There are those who take the train to leave and those who take it to arrive. Then I really do have to leave, he said.

Now that he's left my head is even lighter I feel it flying away with the wind, if you please. I'm thinking of something but my thoughts are uncertain, I don't know precisely what they mean. Maybe I'm sorry. I'll never allow my thoughts to scatter for such a trifle, I must keep them together at all costs.

I feel something empty here and there as if I were lacking something. Instead I'm still all here, you're a whole man don't worry. All right a whole man but

WHAT IS MAN FOR?

Is he useful to somebody? To whom?

I'm walking in the middle of the countryside, there at the end you can see the railroad embankment and there's a train going by but it doesn't make the usual noise. I stop, I listen carefully, and yet this is the train from Latina that goes to Rome, the so-called Littorina it's a real train with passengers looking out of the windows. It was Benito Mussolini who gave it that name.

I remember the sound of the train, I liked it. The sound of the train from the distance. I also liked the trees with the wind whistling through their branches. Must I do something or wait? All this silence, the voice has gone away, I'm glad I mean at heart I'm sorry. It went away crying it cried go ahead and cry, I don't care in the least. When the cold wind bites your ears off, when the sand blows into your eyes. I don't want to think about it. Luckily memory tends to forget.

These old olive trees along the road all together made an olive grove, where are they now I don't see them. I don't even see the olive grove. Isn't it there, or is it me who can't see it? And the copper wires of the High Tension? Is it my fault I don't see you or is it your fault because you're not there? And the Santa Palomba tower with its buzz. They don't make themselves heard any more. Sibelius is keeping quiet too, it's very strange.

I can't see the blue Heavens with their white clouds. Why don't I see the Heavens? All right the Heavens but what about the stones of the Mediaeval Tower they're basalt in other words a very hard volcanic stone. They've been there for centuries, since the Middle Ages. Now it seems to have been torn down. But why do you do these things secretly? And Rome? It's eighteen miles from here everybody can see it, they come on purpose from all parts of the World. You can't tell me Rome isn't there, a whole city. You can see its lights reflected against the clouds. Then the Electric Company is working, that at least.

I see something moving at the end of the road, it seems a little cloud a dog a black automobile a human shadow. No, it's them they've come back from Rome with their wagons and their panther jeeps. One panther has hidden behind the hedge and is waiting for the right moment to leap on me.

They've got me mixed up with somebody who looks like me, you've mixed me up with somebody else who's run away. He took the train for Rome, if you hurry maybe you'll be in time to stop him at the Rome Station when he arrives. If you

[207]

see him crying pay no attention, it's a pretense. If you want a piece of advice take him right away to Regina Coeli. If he talks make him keep quiet.

Meanwhile I walk slowly on to the meadow, cripes instead I'm running. I hear the footsteps of people arriving and then

A VOICE FROM THE DISTANCE.

It comes closer it's behind my back. Luckily nobody is looking at me as I go away. I'm already on the road and I'm walking free and alone like an I don't remember what you call it. I turn and look at all those people in the meadow, maybe it's all beginning again from the beginning. But if you ask me this is really

THE END.